Alfred Hine

London, Leek, Macclesfield, The Potteries, Buxton, The

seasons, The farmers' Calendar,

And other Poems

Alfred Hine

London, Leek, Macclesfield, The Potteries, Buxton, The seasons, The farmers' Calendar,
And other Poems

ISBN/EAN: 9783337158101

Printed in Europe, USA, Canada, Australia, Japan

Cover: Foto ©Andreas Hilbeck / pixelio.de

More available books at **www.hansebooks.com**

ALFRED HINE

LONDON,

LEEK,

MACCLESFIELD,

THE POTTERIES,

BUXTON,

THE SEASONS,

THE FARMERS'
CALENDAR,

AND OTHER POEMS

By Alfred Hine.

PREFACE.

Cheerful, bright and sunny memories, how delightful and pleasant they are. How gladly we welcome them, proving that, to a certain extent, we are happier for having been happy. Still, something more is wanted, mankind the world over, needs also present happiness and enjoyment, and is seeking it in a variety of different ways. Some in love, courtship and marriage find much pleasure when the course of true love runs smooth, pure and honourable; whilst some again may be looking forward to gaining position, wealth, or other attainments, in the future hoping then to be happy. Others wisely seek to improve and enjoy the social and domestic moral and spiritual pleasures and privileges of daily life—seeing the bright and cheerful side of things, and anxious that others also may enjoy the sunshine and pleasures surrounding the path of those who will accept and gather up these sunbeams and blessings. Let us endeavour to comfort and brighten each others' journey through life. If we can innocently amuse, cheer and instruct, those around us, we know it will not be in vain, for we believe in many instances laughter is better than medicine; and, that we need not have a long face in order to be virtuous. Would we reap happiness? let us in faith and hope sow seeds of loving kindness—sow to the spirit "for whatsoever a man soweth, that shall he also reap."

To the parents, children, young men, maidens, husbands and wives of Great Britain may I be permitted humbly to dedicate this small volume of poems, hoping they may prove acceptable, pleasant and profitable, to many.

Yours truly,

ALFRED HINE.

Leekfrith, near Leek.
1897.

A SUBJECT OF INTEREST.

In Eden's fairest garden,
   Its pure primeval bowers,
'Twas even then important
   'Mid sweetest fruits and flowers.

Enchanting as was Eden,
   Rich beauty, fragrance rare,
Man needed a companion,
   Its lovliness to share.

A helpmeet was provided
   To comfort, cheer, relieve,
Young Adam soon decided
   To woo and win Miss Eve.

His offer she accepted,
   Her love to him inclined :
They in due course united
   In marriage—sweetly joined.

Right down the aisle of ages
   All ranks have followed suit :
Peasants and monarchs, sages,
   Did wedlocks ranks recruit.

Our great grandfathers studied
   This interesting theme :
Grandmothers also copied
   Examples they had seen.

We, their descendants, follow ;
   Oft in their footsteps tread,
And take it as good counsel,
   In honour love, woo, wed.

Marriage is still an honour,
   Now as in scripture times,
Let each read, mark, and follow
   Those pure and sacred lines.

3

LOVE, COURTSHIP AND MARRIAGE.

How bright is the home-life, how fresh is the morn
Where love weaves its trelise to deck and adorn ;
When tenderest feelings in harmony blend,
How cheerful and pleasant the charms which they lend.

The birds and the bees, the herbs, fruit and flowers,
How delightful and fragrant in love's sunny hours ;
When young men and maidens now blooming and fair,
Pure love and affection with each other share.

Be equal, seek guidance and help from above,
Ere yet into courtship emerges true love;
In love and in courtship be honest and pure,
In honour endeavour the prize to secure.

How enchanting a walk up hill or through dale,
When mutual affections and feelings prevail ;
The scene most romantic or even maybe
The beauties of nature love helps you to see.

Through forest or glen, when cool or when hot,
How wooers observe the sweet Forget-me-not.
In town or in country pure love is the same,
Still bright are its laurels, and well-deserved fame.

When courtship advances from bloom into fruit
May wedlock's dear link, from branches to root
Be steeped in affection, in honour, in love,
Not transient or fleeting, but firm let it prove.

In sunshine or clouds, in love dwell and abide,
Unitedly steer whatever betide.
Be loving, affectionate, kind, as of yore,
And sail for the harbour of peace evermore.

How sweet is the home-life, how fragrant the flowers,
If love, like a mantle, decks home's sunny bowers ;
Let tenderest affections in harmony blend
In peace, love, and concord, life's honeymoon spend.

4

LOOK AT THE BRIGHT SIDE.

Boys, girls, men and maidens, all favour the right,
Be like the wise people who see what is bright,
In clouds or in sunshine whatever betide
Endeavour your best to see the bright side.

If lengthy and heavy at times be your purse
Don't grumble, remember still things might be worse.
Assist the discouraged, and cheer on the sad,
And win back to virtue the base and the bad.

If short is your purse, and lightish at times,
Yet cheerfully whistle or sing the sweet rhymes;
It isn't much cumber to carry about,
So scatter kind words and looks on your route

Suppose you reside near the top of a hill,
It's steep climbing up, but think if you will,
How sweet and refreshing and pure is the air,
The landscape before you, how pleasant, how fair.

If down in the valley your residence be,
Think how you are favoured; with thankfulness see
The bright side of valleys, how easy to find,
How level to walk, how calm is the wind.

Suppose you reside in the city or town
How pleasant to dwell in a place of renown.
In ancient or modern, or both, it may be,
The useful and bright side of things may you see.

If true love and courtship with you is combined,
And you to each other are fully inclined,
Be equal, be faithful, and ever do right,
In loving and wooing be gentle and bright.

Suppose you've done well, and married a wife,
Or the wife has a husbandman wedded for life.
In peace, love, and concord both ever abide,
In harmony dwelling behold the bright side.

Or, if you are single, don't fret about that,
Your family roofed with one bonnet or hat;
Agree with yourself, to others be kind,
And try in good earnest the bright side to find.

If tired and thirsty, and quite anxious for tea,
The water ice-cold, the fire low it may be,
Add fuel or poke it, and see the bright side,
Wait, patiently wait, until boiling tide.

Employers, employés, should see the bright side,
And, pulling together, contented abide;
Fair wages and profits, each do the right thing,
Uniting your efforts, prosperity bring.

Supposing you drive one, or two, four-in-hand,
The road's rather narrow, or hilly the land,
Gee! whoa! now be steady, still hold to the right,
Attend to your driving, keep cheerful and bright.

If walking in mud, it is soft for the corns,
Far safer than treading on thistles or thorns?
Apply well the water when in comes the tide,
Or brush up and polish, and show the bright side.

If busy at farming, in shop or the mill,
Making shoes or new garments to fit if you will;
Work cheerfully, manfully, brightly, all round,
Admiring the flowers whilst tilling the ground.

Supposing you have leisure time at command,
Improve it well, use it, don't indolent stand ;
Find something to occupy talents and mind,
Endeavour to brighten the lot of mankind.

If riding the cycle, motor car, or balloon,
Be grateful for light of sun, stars or the moon,
Still don't over-run a pure loving mind,
And when you alight be grateful and kind.

If you walk, trot, or gallop, or sail on the sea,
Endeavour at all times pure Christians to be;
The path of true wisdom is bright as the day,
Each find it, and walk it, or run it we say.

Girls, boys, maidens, men, all cling to the right,
Be truly wise people, be cheerful and bright;
Look out for the sunshine, and gladly reside,
In city, town, village, and see the bright side.

HOW TO BE HAPPY.

Be cheerful—neither frown nor fret,
Or shed the tears of vain regret ;
When past mistakes have hurried by,
Except to right them heave no sigh.

Don't only look for flaws in work,
Or dream that all their duties shirk ;
See also what is neat and well,
Your honest admiration tell.

Our neighbours thus to help and cheer
Will do no harm, we need not fear ;
If we can brighten others' lot,
Some beams may fall on our own plot.

Don't meet the troubles yet to come,
Or be morose and sour at home ;
But open, frank and friendly be,
To all be kind, in peace agree.

Don't look for clouds, or storms, or wind,
But if they come, be patient, kind ;
The silver lining try to see,
And thankful for your mercies be.

7

HOW TO BE HAPPY—*continued.*

Don't upon one weak human back
Past, present, and the future pack ;
But cast your care on One above
Of matchless power— of boundless love.

Find wisdom's happy, pleasant ways,
And travel in them all your days ;
So shall your life be happy, bright—
At morning, noon and evening light.

Don't give harsh words and looks, or frowns,
Dwellers in country, hamlets, towns ;
Be loving, kind, and cheer the sad,
Be sunny, cheerful, happy, glad.

A NORTHERN TOUR.

Tourists from pleasant town of Leek,
Who rural rustic pleasures seek,
May find a Northern drive or walk
Attractive, with kind friends to talk.

Not far from Leek is Rudyard vale,
'Mid scenery of hill and dale ;
The Switzerland of Staffordshire
Full well deserves a passing lyre.

When Winter's frost has bound the lake,
Skaters may go, for gliding's sake;
In spring and summer sailing go
Ply well the oars and onward row,

Then onward, take train, wheel, or drive,
Until at Rushton you arrive;
Green pastures, Corn, and Meadow land,
Doth admiration there command.

A NORTHERN TOUR — *continued.*

On up the side of river Dane,
It's charms we need not here explain;
It must be seen to understand
Its rustic beauty on each hand.

View Swythamley, a calm retreat,
An ancient hall, a country seat,
Ludchurch's rugged rocks behold,
Where heather's blooming charms unfold.

Gradbach, about one mile from here,
Examine next, as on you steer;
Then past Newstone, and Middle Hills,
Where fresh sweet breeze the air oft fills.

Then Upper Hulme and Blackshaw Moor,
Walk, drive, or run the cycles o'er;
For rest and pure refreshment seek
Again the Moorland town of Leek.

FAREWELL OLD YEAR.

Farewell old year thy days have sped,
Thy summer hours have past and fled;
Thy clouds have hastened o'er the sky.
So now old year we'll say "good-bye."

Farewell to thy sweet flowers and fruits:
Thy breezy morn and eve's salute,
The merry song of birds and bees,
Warbling their music in the trees.

Farewell thy seed and harvest tide.
How swiftly past thy seasons glide!
Thy summer's heat and winter's snow
How rapidly they come and go!

9

Farewell harsh words, better left unsaid,
How oft they caused us tears to shed !
We well can spare you, go and stay,
And never come again we say.

Kind words, we'll scarcely bid farewell,
For still in memory's track they dwell ;
They cause no aching heart or sigh,
No tear drop's start, no weeping eye.

Kind actions stay, don't haste away,
But spring up fresh some future day ;
We really must not say farewell,
For close by you we wish to dwell.

Farewell old year we grieve that we
No better use have made of thee;
But hope if spared to say farewell,
Again, through grace, good news to tell.

HUSBANDS AND WIVES.

Once on a time, a bridegroom,
   After the knot was tied,
Walked out into the garden,
   With his new loving bride.

And threw a line right over
   Their rural cottage roof,
A rope, which was well able
   To give their strength full proof.

Giving his wife the one end.
   He went round to the other,
And he pulled hard at his side,
   Whilst she pulled at the other.

Then he cried "pull it over"
"I can't" his wife replied,
And so, just while she rested,
　Round to her side he hied.

And then they pulled together,
　The husband and his bride,
And o'er it came quite easy,
　When they pulled side by side.

Said he "how hard our labour,
　Tugging against each other,
How easy and how pleasant,
　When we both pull together."

So stepping on together,
　Through good report or ill,
Ever remember courtship,
　And when you said "I will."

Each wear their loving manners,
　Around their own fireside,
As smoothly passing onward,
　The time doth sweetly glide.

And if a cloud arises
　Across the bright blue sky,
Still gently pull together,
　'Twill vanish bye and bye.

If anything should happen
　To ruffle either one,
In wisdom just be silent
　Until the temper 's gone.

Still let a Christ-like spirit
　Choose what may go or come,
Be everywhere presented
　But most of all at home.

E'er pulling both together,
  In loving union sweet,
Until, in fairer climates,
  Before the throne they meet.

HOMES OF ENGLAND.

Fair favoured homes of England,
  In towns, farmhouse and halls,
Sweet love and peace o'ershadow you
  From floor to roof and walls.

In village, cottage, hamlets,
  Let those who there reside
In Christian love and temperance
  E're pleasantly abide.

Husbands and wives and children,
  Together sweetly pull ;
Home comforts and the larder
  Replenished be, and full.

May deeds right noble ever
  Adorn our English homes,
And gentle loving kindness
  Dictate both words and tones.

Let strife and discord never
  An entrance gain or find :
Each one through grace exhibit
  A calm and Christian mind.

And strive to make home's fireside
  The brighest spot on earth ;
Of useful aspirations
  The cradle and the birth.

Let prayer and scripture teaching
　　Show wisdom and true worth ;
Break forth in dear old home life
　　In Christian songs of mirth.

Dear, cheerful homes of England,
　　Farmhouse, or towns, or hall :
Let Christian faith, love, temperance,
　　Admission gain to all.

LIKE, AND YET UNLIKE.

Husbands and wives, e'er strive to be
　　Like music—calm and sweet ;
Unlike the mighty organ's roar,
　　Or surges of the deep.

Let them be like transparent glass,
　　Each other's motives see :
But not like glass to crack or break,—
　　Love's union, strong and free.

Be like an echo—gentle, kind,
　　Replying to kind words :
Unlike an echo harsh and gruff,
　　If one gives angry words.

Or like the snail, be mostly found
　　About your own home tracks,
Unlike the snail, please do not try
　　To over-load your backs.

Be like a sunbeam, bright and clear,
　　In pleasant month of May :
But never let the little clouds
　　Chase cheerfulness away.

13

Be like the merry honey bee—
   Draw sweetness from the flowers ;
But unlike the bee when angry,
   Stinging with all its powers.

Or like the ancient village clock —
   Good time and order keep ;
Unlike the clock, don't speak so loud
   But why your friends can sleep.

Be like a fine warm day in June--
   Let love be all a-glow ;
Unlike a dull November day
   Of fog, or frost, or snow.

Then kindly help each other on,
   Like pilgrims on life's way :
Ere tending to the better land
   Of pure and perfect day.

SUMMER.

Hail ! Summer, bright with pleasant hours,
The air perfumed with fruit and flowers ;
So lovely and so dainty they,
We could enjoy their longer stay.

In town and country, summer bright
Is pleasant with its radiant light :
The merry notes of birds and bees,
And rich green foliage on the trees.

The cattle seek the grateful shade,
Or in the cooling waters wade ;
While fowls are basking in the sand,
The wild flowers deck the meadow-land.

SUMMER—*continued.*

The farmer and his chosen men
Go forth in early morning, when
The dewdrops glisten on the blades,
And down they cut the grass in swathes.

Anon the sun arises high,
And quickly it doth warm and dry
The men and maidens, ted and row,
The grass which yesterday did grow.

They work it well in glowing sun,
The harvest work must needs be done :
And then, ere falls the shades of night,
They cob it up in lumps so light.

The next day shake it in the breeze ;
In harvest time be busy please :
While sun is shining make good hay,
Before the wet and stormy day.

When it is ready, pitch it up—
And quench your thirst in temperance cup—
Drive on, gee ! ho ! for hay-loft floor,
And move it well from pitch-hole door'

And so from Monday morning's dawn
'Till Saturday at evening's fall,
Be making progress day by day,
And when quite ready, cart dry hay.

Let each in towns and country, then,
Improve the summer time : that when
Our summers and our autumns past,
We may have rest in heaven at last.

Hail ! glad, glad summer, bright and gay,
With air redolent with new hay ;
The sun rides on in sky so bright,
And long delays the shade of night.

AUTUMN.

Come Autumn, when the Summer 's gone,
The trees with luscious fruit upon :
Ripe pears and apples, plum or cherry,
Quite useful fruit to make us merry.

The hedgerows decked with wild fruit gay,
As lovely as in merry May ;
With hazelnuts and blackberries bright,
And raspberries sweet, rich, and ripe.

The seeds which had been sown in spring
Have sprung aloft as if on wings :
When warmed and watered from above,
In act responded to God's love.

And lo ! behold rich harvest fields,
Which food for man and beast doth yield,
Is swaying gently in the breeze,
Whilst feathered songsters feed at ease.

For corn and wheat doth ripen fast,
The promised harvest comes at last ;
Men come with hooks and horse-machines
Without command of kings or queens.

In every land, and realm, and clime,
Cut down the grain in harvest time ;
And bind in sheaves so plump and round,
Then fix the kivers on the ground.

When fielded well, and firm and dry,
Come, men, with carts and waggons hie :
Drive on your horses, cart away,
Don't linger on fine harvest days :

But haste and get it garnered in
Before the winter snows begin ;
When safely gathered from the ground,
Dales, hills, with harvest home resound.

AUTUMN—*continued.*

To God, the giver of all good,
Whose gracious promise firm has stood
Seed time and harvest, day and night,
Still onward march and go all right ;

To Him our choicest anthems sing,
And grateful heart-felt homage bring :
Thankful again for harvest store,
Now safely garnered in once more.

Old Autumn now will soon be gone :
Sweet flowers, and trees with fruit upon,
Ripe cherries, apples, plums, and pears ;
Will pass and go like former years.

WINTER.

Behold ! grand old Winter is now at our door,
The days are so short—soon the sunshine is o'er ;
The fog settles thick, and the mists on the hills,
And the waters rush on down the rippling rills.

Still onward they run o'er pebbles and sand,
Nor turn back to look for old winter at hand ;
Anon they run calmly through valleys and plains,
Forgetting at present their murmuring strains.

The snow flakes fall fast and thick on the ground,
Soon covering the grass and the herbage there found ;
And cattle and horses must quickly be housed—
Taken in from the pastures on which they have browsed.

But there's hay in the barn   or stack it may be
In loftyish heaps, we are quite pleased to see ;
And with water to drink, corn and hay they may eat,
So we hope they won't grumble, but think it a treat.

WINTER—*continued.*

And then when king frost claims the rivers and lakes,
Young people some pleasure in skating will take ;
While some of us further advanced in years,
Prefer a place near to the fire with our chairs.

When Christmas approaches, the Yule log we take
And place it right up at the back of the grate ;
Tho' there be snow on the ground and frost in the air,
We begin to feel cosy and warm in our chair.

Friend Christmas, we rather delight in thy name,
And with us roast beef and plum pudding have fame ;
The time is right merry, dear friends often meet,
And brothers and sisters each other do greet.

With Christmas long past, snows quickly assuage,
And king frost will also be breaking with age ;
The sun gathers strength as the days grow in length,
And soon we may hail the spring in its zenith.

The ploughman goes forth with dapple and gray,
And he cheerfully steadies the plough right away,
As upwards and downwards, from morning till night,
He turns the new furrows to the left and the right.

So now, for the present, old winter, good-bye,
To meet thy more genial successor we'll hie ;
Sometime when comes Christmas again with good cheer
Most likely friend winter will also be there.

———

SPRING.

Come on, lovely Spring, we welcome thee here :
A hearty good greeting from far and from near :
In towns and in country we love thee alike,
And gladly we linger amidst thy delights.

SPRING—*continued.*

The trees which but recently naked appeared,
Are putting forth buds, and soon will be geared ;
The flowers, which in winter appeared to be dead,
Are springing and growing again on their bed.

The birds, which just twittered and hopped along,
Are getting quite merry with anthem and song ;
And tired of a lonely and solitary state,
Appear now in favour of choosing a mate.

The grass, which in winter was covered with snow,
Behold in its verdure commencing to grow ;
With sunshine and showers, so quickly it springs,
There soon will be quite a nice pasture for things.

The cattle now shortly may take a walk out,
And have a nice taste of fresh grass round about :
The butter and cheese, now rather small store,
Will soon be increasing and growing to more.

The farmer goes forth the good seed to sow,
With well-measured steps both steady and slow ;
He scatters the seed to the left and the right—
In hopes of a harvest both golden and bright.

We love thee, sweet spring, with thy bright sunny hours,
The music of birds and the fragrance of flowers ;
May we, as we pleasantly travel along,
Each join in the chorus with praise and with song.

Come, then, lovely spring, we welcome thee here,
A right hearty greeting from far and from near ;
In towns and in country may each one have light
To prepare for the spring of heaven so bright.

MAY.

Hail! merry May, with wealth of flowers,
And cheerful, pleasant sunny hours;
Though always coming once a year,
Thou art thrice welcome, never fear.

The children think, with youthful glee,
What jolly times they have in thee—
Thy days so fine, and warm, and dry,—
The nests of birds they'll find, or try.

Playing at marbles, ball, or cricket,
Or plucking flowers from hawthorn thicket;
Their leisure moments quickly pass
Amongst wild daisies, flowers and grass.

Whilst with the men and maidens grown,
The darts of Cupid oft are thrown;
Anon they whisper to each other
As sweet as any friend or brother.

What wonder if, in pleasant May,
Some "pop the question," as they say;
The days are long, the sun is bright;
We hope they tie the knot all right.

With this accomplished, still there's more—
If happiness must be the store:
When May and June have passed away,
Be kind and loving every day.

In towns and hamlets, sunny May
Is quite a treat in its own way;
Looked forward to long ere it come,
And well enjoyed till past and gone.

The farmer, during snow and frost,
Looks forth to May, and counts the cost
In provender of hay and corn,
Ere out they go, both hoof and horn.

MAY—*continued.*

Before, and when thou meet'st their gaze,
Let young and old together praise—
Acknowledge God in all their ways,
Throughout bright May and all their days.

Hail! joyous May, with springing flowers,
And genial, bright, and sunny hours;
Though ever coming once a year,
Thou still art welcome, never fear.

GOOD MORN NEW YEAR.

Good morn, new year, we're glad to meet,
In rural walks or crowded street:
May we upon thy pure white page,
Place actions worthy of the age.

We're glad to see thee spruce and gay,
As on thy former natal day,
If man could bear his age as well,
What wonders he would see and tell.

May we improve thee while we may,
For with us long thou wilt not stay,
Thy cheerful, genial, pleasant hours,
Just use them, while they still are ours.

And shun the rock on which we split
During the year we've just seen flit:
If we must triumph in the fray
We must, through grace, keep watch and pray.

In all we think, or do, or say,
Let us march on the good old way:
Which saints of other days have trod,
With peace and joy and grace well shod.

MAY—*continued.*

And as thy days and weeks pass by,
May we be faithful and employ
Our time and talents as we should
Wish when we come to Jordan's flood.

Good morn, new year, we gladly greet
Thee ere thou beat a quick retreat ;
May we, upon thy pure white page,
Plant actions worthy of a sage.

OLD ENGLAND DEAR.

Old England dear, we love thee well,
We are not tired with thee to dwell ;
Let others roam o'er land and sea,
A home on Britain's shores for me.

Thy wide, fair fields, of verdant green,
With flowers and shrubs studded between,
Thy orchards of sweet, rich, ripe fruit,
And hedgerows, vocal with birds' lute.

Thy homestead joys are passing sweet,
Dear wife and children parents meet
And brothers, sisters, there they dwell,
Dear grand old home we love thee well.

Thy Institutions great and free,
Bright home of peace and liberty ;
Here Queen Victoria lives and reigns
A subject of the King of Queens.

Empress of India's foreign strand
And Queen of Britain's happy land ;
Long may she reign, in peace and love,
Guided with wisdom from above.

OLD ENGLAND DEAR—*continued.*

The bible words of grace and truth,
Are read and loved by age and youth :
Its sacred pages shew the way,
Through native land, to realms of day.

Thy Christian Sabbath's gospel preached,
Redemption's story free for each :
Freedom to worship where we please :
In cathedral or mountain breeze,

Hail ! England dear, we love to tell
How pleased we are in thee to dwell ;
Though others roam o'er land and seas,
A home for us in Britain, please.

WHAT'S THE TIME ?

Children, what's the time of day ?
Let me ask you while you play,
Time, if playing with your kite,
Not to hold the string too tight ;
Or if marbles be the game,
Shoot quite straight and take good aim ;
Or if you've a round at cricket,
Roll the ball straight for the wicket.

Children, what's the time of day ?
Listen to me while I say,
If you play at hide-and-seek,
When you're hiding do not speak :
When you're swinging on the gate,
Do not fall and hurt your pate ;
Or if skating on the ice,
Try to glide on safe and nice.

WHAT'S THE TIME—*continued*.

Children, what's the time of day?
Please permit me now to say,
When your holiday's are o'er,
And you go to school once more,
When you read, and write, and spell,
Try your best to do it well;
And in Latin, Greek, and Grammar,
Speak it plain and do not stammer.

Children, what's the time of day?
Please allow me now to say,
Choose if the day is hot or cool,
I hope you go to Sabbath school;
And as you read, and mark, and learn
The chart of life, oh! may you turn
From every form of wrong and sin,
And trusting Jesus, victory win.

Children, what's the time of day?
Don't be impatient while I say,
At morn and eve when you're at home,
May you oft hear the words "well done."
Obedient, loving, true, and kind,
Always the path of duty find;
What you can do for others, see,
And try how useful you can be,

Children, what's the time of day?
Just once again now let me say,
When at your play or at the school,
Whoever may be hot or cool,
At Sabbath school and when at home,
Let all you do be nobly done;
May you have grace from day to day
To shew to each the Christian way.

DON'T GRUMBLE.

We think it unwise to grumble or fret
About that and the other, and do not forget
It never does good, and it often does harm
For to pull a long face—well it hasn't a charm.

Some grumble because they are upon the hill,
The wind often blows—in fact seldom is still,
And it's hard work to walk up the mountain side;
They would rather by far in the valley reside.

Our friends in the valley, they do not forget
That the waters rush down from the hills even yet,
And the land in the valley is sopping with rain,
If they'd a farm on the mountain they wouldn't complain.

The landowner grumbles his tenant's too bad,
The land so neglected makes him to feel sad,
If he farmed it himself complaining he'll say:
Much more than his tenant he'd make it to pay.

The tenant complains his landlord's too near,
He will scarcely find timber the gates to repair;
Was he just the owner they quickly should see
What a capital man with his tenant he'd be.

In towns people grumble the air is not pure,
They would like to reside in the country, that's sure,
A snug house and garden at the foot of the hill,
Where they would not be bothered with gas and its bill.

The shopkeeper thinks there's too much competition,
He finds it too hard to make good provision,
A trade in the country would do him no harm,
For there he might find in his business some charm.

The gentleman driving his coach and his pair,
He grumbles and thinks the roads are unfair
They should be wider in this place, and better in that,
And the mountains and hills he would like to be flat.

DON'T GRUMBLE—*continued.*

Our friend who is walking would gladly ascend
Behind the proud span, his journey to end ;
He wouldn't fret at the road whether hilly or flat,
If he could roll on at a speed such as that.

The people who ride on the cycles they find
There is far too much mud on the road, to their mind ;
And then when they come to the foot of the hill,
They have to dismount and push if you will.

If riding by rail, motor car, or balloon,
They grumble their journey is ended too soon.
Or you must remember it's safer to stand
With your feet firmly planted on fair English land.

In fact its no matter where some people be,
Whether driving on land, or ploughing the sea.
Employers of labour, or they who're employed,
They'll manage to grumble, whatever betide,

Then let us forsake the grumbling trade,
And ever be thankful to him who has made
The richest provisions, our needs to supply,
And purchased a passport to Canaan on high.

So ever remember don't grumble or fret,
About this and the other, and do not forget,
It never does good, but it often does harm,
For to pull a long face— well, it hasn't a charm.

MARKET DAY AT LEEK.

Leek, May, 1897.

The town of Leek, of which we rhyme,
Is quite a busy place :
We greet it now in modern times
Not ancient history trace.

MARKET DAY AT LEEK *continued.*

The shops appear in cheerful garb,
    In sunny pleasant May,
The colours various, superb,
    On Moorland market day.

From far and near they flock to town,
    Some drive, and others walk,
Wednesday at Leek is still renowned ;
    Some come to see and talk.

Others with eggs and butter stand,
    Now butter trade is slow,
Supply is greater than demand
    Causing it to be low.

Some Wednesdays, after standing hours,
    Price, tenpence, nine or eight,
It trys the farmer's patient powers,
    The cash is not much weight.

Though cash comes in but slow, we fear,
    Some rather over load,
When leaving town they scarce can steer,
    Quite straight along the road.

Let town and country friends be wise,
    And never over load :
Or else they will not gain a prize,
    For walking street or road.

Each take the pathway, pure and right,
    And help each other on,
Make market days still grow more bright,
    While passing one by one.

Dear Moorland town, we wish thee well,
    May trade improve abound ;
Prosperity within thee dwell
    Spreading the country round.

MARKET DAY AT LEEK—*continued*.

The present, in these busy days,
    Engages much our time :
Still, possibly, some future lays,
    May deal with " Auld lang syne."

BUXTON.

In Derbyshire, famed for its peaks,
Its bold aspiring mountain steeps,
Romantic is the scenery there,
Fresh is the breeze—the landscape fair.

Stands Buxton, healthy, pleasant place,
There visitors find welcome space.
Vast numbers visit Buxton town,
Now quite a scene of fame—renown.

Its healthy springs have useful been,
To peasants, nobles. and to queen.
Were highly prized in days of yore,
And are at present, more and more.

Buildings substantial, stately, grand,
Buxton adorn on either hand ;
Chaste architectural beauty rare,
Is prominently portrayed there.

Gardens. pavilion, concert hall,
Sweet strains of music rise and fall,
Upon the ear, delightful. sweet,
Harmoniously—a real treat.

The Serpentine, and other walks,
Where tourists often stroll and talk,
'Mid pleasant woodlands, shrubs and trees.
The public have admission free.

BUXTON—*continued.*

Away from there, about one mile,
Two truant lovers leapt in style—
The open gulf in safety past,
And their pursuers left at last.

Buxton is worthy of its fame,
Inside and out, through street and lane:
The scenery 's romantic—fair,
May poor and rich its beauties share.

ODE TO AN OLD FRIEND.

Hail! Grandfather's clock, i'th' corner,
How thou points our memories back
To the sunny hours of childhood,
With thy merry tick, tick, tack.

How we used to look in wonder,
At the fingers on thy face,
And it puzzled us to find out
How our friends the time could trace.

Bye-and-bye we learned to count thee,
As thou struck'st the hours of day,
But to tell how many minutes
Was above our childhood's way.

Thou kept'st time and still kept ticking,
When we mis-improv'd our time :
Oft we did not do our duty
Half as well as thou did'st thine.

Even when we did some mischief,
Thou kept'st ticking striking time,
And we must confess our conduct
Was not near as right as thine.

ODE TO AN OLD FRIEND—*continued.*

We had many pleasant seasons,
While thou still kept'st beating time,
And when near to bed-time drawing,
We'd have liked thee stop awhile.

But thou would'st not wait a minute,
Rallying, ticking, tacking on,
And our play must quickly finish
When the time allowed was gone.

Thou mad'st progress when our parents
In the twilight turned the key,
Gently taught to say "Our Father,"
And to pray with bended knee.

Then when mother kindly tucked us,
And she kissed us sweet good-night,
Thou went on as fresh as ever,
Both in darkness and in light.

When we awoke in morning's beauty,
Be it six, seven, eight or nine,
Still thou wast not shirking duty,
We could hear thee striking time.

And we hurried down to breakfast,
Sheepish, shy when after nine,
But thou seemed to take no notice,
For thou wast not needing thine.

Then at times in youthful frolic,
We should fall slap on the floor,
Still thou kept'st as grave as ever,
Going on just as before.

When at times we rode in triumph,
On our brother, shoulder height:
Even this did not surprise thee,
Thou kept'st ticking, right and straight.

ODE TO AN OLD FRIEND—*continued*.

If we played at "rags-a-bundle,"
Blythly laughing, going round ;
If we even chanced to tumble.
Still when time thy bell would sound.

When we'd grown in years and wisdom,
And could tell thy minute time,
Though we highly prized the knowledge.
Still it did not alter thine.

Faithful old-time friend remind us
To improve the present time,
Building on the Rock of Ages.
'Till we reach a brighter clime.

THE SNOWDROP.

Hail Snowdrop! pure and hardy flower,
    'Midst snow and frost thy modest head
Reminds us of fair Eden's bowers,
    Of which we've often heard and read.

Welcome first of the new year's flowers,
    In sheltered vale or old ditch side,
Thy rich green stem, and pure white flower,
    Comes while the winter here abides.

Thy drooping humble, graceful form,
    At once, sweet, gentle, fresh and gay,
Cheers us amidst old winter's storm.
    Patient to wait for brighter days.

May we, like thee, be pure and white,
    Washed in the cleansing precious blood.
Which ages back, on Calvary's height,
    For all was spilt a healing flood.

31

THE SNOWDROP—*continued*.

Sinners, through faith in Christ, may gain
    Pure garments, whiter than the snow,
By washing in the crimson tide,
    Which from His wounded side did flow.

Let each now to the fountain come,
    In David's house still open wide.
Come rich and poor, come bond and free,
    And wash, by faith, in Calvary's tide.

Come all of every race and tribe,
    A ransom full, for you was wrought.
Gentile and Jew, come freely take
    The pardon on Mount Calvary bought.

Purer than snow or snowdrop keep
    May we, through grace, bear fruit and flowers,
Through cloud or sunshine's journey steep,
    Aspiring to fair Canaan's bowers.

HAPPY DAYS.

Let's talk about our happy days,
    Forgetting all the sad ones :
We each have cause for thankfulness
    That we've so many glad ones.

For pleasant hours and loving friends,
    Food and shelter, clothes to wear,
Genial sunshine, gentle showers,
    And abundance of fresh air.

Thank the Giver of all good :
    For God's holy Book to read,
Full instruction what to do,
    What to say, and what we need.

Let each search its sacred pages,
    Diligently mark and learn ;
Truest wisdom of all ages,
    Council how and when to turn ;

Turn to Him who says so kindly :
    "Come . . . . and I will give you rest" ;
They who love Him, they who trust Him,
    Happy are, and truly blest,

Thankful for our Sabbath schools,
    Where we learn the pleasant way
To a home more bright and fair—
    Home of everlasting day,

Thankful for the cup that cheers,
    For a cup of social tea,
Where we meet with friends again
    Whom we're very pleased to see.

Let's talk about our happy days,
    Just skipping all the sad ones :
We each have cause for thankfulness
    For quite a host of glad ones.

LEEK PAST AND PRESENT.

Tune *Auld Lang Syne*.

Metropolis of the Moorlands,
    Of thee we gladly speak ;
Fair bulwark of our native land,
    Hail ! ancient town of Leek.

For centuries thy worthy fame
    Has stood the test of time,
And Leke, or Leek, has been thy name
    Since days of Auld Lang Syne.

LEEK PAST AND PRESENT—*continued.*

What stirring scenes have taken place
   In days of ancient yore,
It would, of course, take too much space
   To con them fully o'er.

In days of old if dames grew warm,
   The Churnet kept quite cool :
We hope it did their health no harm
   Whilst in the ducking-stool.

The grumbling tongue might have a rest,
   From angry language cease ;
A time, at least, those they opprest
   Might spend in quiet peace.

Perhaps the gents at times, as well,
   Deserved a cooling bath,
Thus teaching them 'tis wise to dwell
   In peace, avoiding wrath.

But now the ducking-stool and pranks
   Are things of distant past ;
Their services dispensed, with thanks,
   They've long aside been cast.

In Leek did Johnson's father as
   Apprentice serve his time
With Mr. Joseph Needham learn
   In Days of Auld Lang Syne.

Through Leek the young Pretender came
   With his Scotch army past ;
No doubt his visit and his name
   O'er Leek a gloom would cast

Leek had her own brave, noble sons,
   And daughters, too, of old ;
The deeds of many famous ones
   Will often be re-told.

LEEK PAST AND PRESENT —*continued,*

Now, gliding down to present times,
  Leek friends we gladly greet ;
In conversation or in rhymes
  We're pleased with you to meet.

Your famous silk, may it be worn
  By ladies, far and near ;
The town and country well adorn,
  Numbers in silk appear.

Your groceries and bread, and beef,
  Right useful they are found ;
Often affording much relief,
  May customers abound.

The friends in Leek with pleasure see
  Our country folks in town,
For they fresh eggs and butter need,
  And cheese of good renown.

The farmers well enjoy a drive
  Through country lanes to town,
They sometimes need a coat or vest,
  Ladies require a gown.

From many miles around they come,
  Some produce bring— to sell.
Others to look about them come,
  And hear the news— or tell.

When driving home, the landscape fair
  Stretching on either hand
With gentle breeze and pure fresh air—
  Attention doth demand.

Metropolis of the Moorlands,
  The purest pleasures seek,
And find, and still in honour stand,
  Fair favoured town of Leek.

35

FLOWERS.

Sweet flowers of summer months and spring,
Come, and your fragrant beauty bring ;
So innocent, so gentle, pure,
A hearty welcome you insure.

Pure, lovely Violets, white and blue,
Sweet Williams, too, we're pleased to view ;
The Candytuft, so gentle, sweet ;
Wallflowers, with fragrance quite a treat.

Consider Lilies—how they grow :
They toil not, neither spin nor sow ;
Yet the wise king was not arrayed
In raiment pure as these display.

Daisies and Buttercups, as well,
Forget-me-nots, and bright Bluebell,
Sweetbrier, and Crab, and Hawthorne bloom,
Display their colours pretty soon.

The cultivated orchard trees
Show their fresh bloom as well as these ;
And when arrived to ripe rich fruit :
Pleasant to taste, 'mid birds salute.

Sweet Mignonette and London Pride,
Poppies and pansies by their side ;
The Lupin and the tall Sunflower
Towering aloft in garden bower.

The queen of flowers please don't forget,
But let it crown the garden yet :
The virgin, charming, lovely rose,
How fragrant underneath the nose.

Sweet flowers of summer, autumn, spring,
Let us still of your beauty sing :
So pleasant, innocent, and gay,
You are quite welcome, we will say.

LEEKFRITH VALLEY.

Hail ! charming valley of Leekfrith,
We think of thee much gladness with :
Cradled the Roach and Gun between,
And mantled with rich verdant green.

A snug and quiet rural place :
Vast numbers of the human race
Have not yet been to view it o'er,
In modern times, or years of yore.

The talk about the Puffing-bills,
Which should have run between the hills
From Macclesfield to town of Leek.
Seems quiet gone, as if to sleep.

But though at present fallen down,
Still try until success doth crown ;
And through thee swiftly trains shall glide
On which we'd gladly take a ride.

In childhood, we had many a fall
Upon thy grass, from hedge and wall ;
But, like the valiant knights of old,
Rose up again, ere we were told.

So let thy railway project, rise,
For lying still will earn no prize ;
Then up again, and progress make,
And off to market people take.

Still down thy centre runs the brook
O'er which, in youth, some leaps we took ;
And in its limpid waters caught
Some bonny, brightly spotted trout.

There country boys have often bathed.
And in its sparkling waters laved ;
Away from bustle, strife, and din,
The Leekfrith Valley dwelling in.

LEEKFRITH VALLEY *continued.*

The cattle there have quench'd their thirst,
'Tis long, long ages, since the first
Partook its waters, cool and clear,
Gathering from springs both far and near.

Not far from this bright, rippling brook,
The village stands called Meerbrook—
A snug and cosy country place,
The scene of many a school boys' race.

Two sanctuarys there are found,
In which the country people round
May hear the gospel preached and read,
If they fair Zion's courts will tread.

But some who dwell in Leekfrith vale,
To attend God's house do often fail;
Come, and a hearty welcome find,
Trust, serve the Saviour of mankind.

Come, all beneath the radiant sun,
Along with all 'twixt Roach and Gun;
To Jesus turn, believe and live,
To Him all praise and honour give.

Join any sanctuary where
The gospel's read and published there;
In prayer and praise be often found,
While marching to fair Canaan's ground.

Still, lovely valley of Leekfrith,
We muse of thee much pleasure with;
Sloping high, Roach and Gun between,
Deck'd with sweet flowers and herbage green.

THE BIBLE.

The Bible—sacred word of truth :
Safe guide for old, mid'-age, and youth,
Let all explore its holy page,
In every clime of every age ;
Its history—faithful, true. and good,
Before, and at, and since the Flood.
Man's character's depicted there
Untarnished, honest, strictly fair ;
Creation's story there is told :
Long years ago, in days of old,
Jehovah spake, and it was done,
Earth, sea, and firmament, and sun,
Birds, beasts and fishes, moon and stars,
With Saturn, Jupiter, and Mars,
Sweet flowers and grasses, shrubs and trees,
With insects, flies, and humming bees,
Crowning creaton's wonderous plan
With God's most noble creature—man.
Planted in Eden's lovely bowers,
'Midst choicest fruits and virgin flowers,
A helpmeet was provided man,
So Adam's Eve was called "woman" ;
And while they loved and served their God,
Sweet Eden's walks together trod—
How pleasant, happy, was the state
Of man, and of his loving mate,
Their heavenly Father served, adored,
Conforming to His will and word ;
But as the sacred book we read
How our first parents disobeyed—
Partook of the forbidden fruit,
Losing of purity the root ;
How sad, that to temptation's power
They yielded in that fatal hour,
And thus entailed such sad disgrace
Upon themselves and on our race ;
Thus wandered from sweet love and truth,
God sent them out of Eden forth
To till the ground and sow the seed,

THE BIBLE—*continued*.

And labour hard to earn their bread.
The years did quickly come and go,
The time to reap, the time to sow,
Long generations past and went,
Mankind their days in evil spent :
The paths of evil sought and trod,
Brought on the deluge—mighty flood :
Proving, if man must victory win,
He must not tread the paths of sin.
God's faithful promise still stands good,
Recorded after Noah's flood,
Seedtime and harvest, day and night,
They do not cease, but go all right ;
Also the promised rainbows bend—
Continues still at times to lend
Pure glowing colours, bright and gay,
Near morning hours or close of day.
The laws of God—pure, just, and good,
Which have for generations stood,
Spoken upon mount Sinai's height,
Binding on all, both day and night.
How great a change would soon appear,
If all by Bible laws would steer :
Our doors we should not need to lock,
Afraid of others taking stock ;
Our police force might then disband,
Might plough, and sow, and till the land ;
Our judges, juries, prisons, be
Dispensed with thanks, we'd gladly see ;
The spears and swords the smiths might beat,
When they arrived at wielding heat,
To implements to till the ground,
And so their usefulness abound.
The prophesies of ancient seers,
In holy scripture, too, appears,
The Holy Spirit them inspired
To tell events which should transpire :
Forward with eye of faith they looked
To Him, who human nature took—

THE BIBLE. — continued.

The Mighty Counsellor and guide
Through life, o'er Jordan's swelling tide.
In scripture we've redemption's story,
How Christ, King of eternal glory,
Came from the shining ranks above—
So vast, so infinite, His love—
To seek and save man's fallen race,
With richest plentitude of grace:
Suffered and died on Calvary's tree
To set the ransomed nations free.
Salvation's purchased for mankind,
Sinners, through Christ, may mercy find:
Then turn, repent, believe, and live.
To Him both heart and life now give,
Come all to Christ, and find sweet rest,
Trust in Him, and be truly blest;
Balm, healing, for the broken heart.
The oil of joy for ache and smart.
There's on the Bible's sacred page,
Instructions for all ranks and age:
Servants and Masters, husband, wife,
Pure guide to peace and happy life,
Parents and children, brothers, friends,
Pointing to Him who freely sends
His help and blessing and rich grace
To those who run the Christian race;
For cottagers, for kings and queens,
Tradesmen, or dukes, with those between:
Directions to the good old way,
Leading to realms of brightest day.
Grand Bible words of sacred truth,
Shewing sure path for age or youth,
Guide us, as with an Angel's hand,
Through Christ alone to promised land.
There's peace and happiness in store
For Jesu's followers ever more;
Joy, love and pleasures here below,
Bright crowns and harps where comes no woe.

A SUMMER WALK.

How verdant the grass in bright, sunny June,
How cheerful and jovial the Linnet's sweet tune,
As out in the fields and the meadows we walked
With the dear little children, who chatted and talked.

They gathered the flowers, and questions they asked
Which at times our powers of language quite taxed :
How the grasses and herbs and the flowers did grow,
And who planted them there to bloom and to glow.

When, as we walked onward, the Finch and the Lark
Were warbling so blithely, the children said " Hark ! "
What pleasure and gladness the little birds bring,
Who taught them so sweetly to twitter and sing ?

We pointed them upwards to clouds and to sun,
And told them the moon and the stars they did run
The courses oppointed at God's good command,
And all things are kept and sustained by His hand.

VALUE THE TIME.

In life's early morning, in manhood's full prime,
Whatever your station, still value the time ;
And as it advances, still use it aright,
That so all your hours may be cheerful and bright.

At home or abroad, at school or at play,
Still follow the council of Jesus the Way ;
And when you are reading, and writing, and summing,
Still seek to improve for the time that is coming.

When school days are over, and time's flying fast,
Still strive to engage in the pleasures that last ;
Abstain from the puffing in which some engage,
Nor dream it will make you as wise as a sage.

And think it not manly to drink of the glass
Which brings sorrow at present, and woes at the last ;
For wine is a mocker, so be not deceived,
But always abstain, and thus be relieved.

Get honest employment while yet you are young,
And don't let the colt shirk the collar too long :
For many grow wilful and stubborn with age,
And object to the harness, from noble to page.

Attend to your business from morning till night :
What your hand finds to do, ever do with your might,
And leave unto others to pine or to fret
That they still have the ladder to climb even yet.

Then pull off your coat, and roll up your sleeves—
Work hard for yourselves, help others in need,
Push with your shoulders, and turn the wheel round,
In mill or in workshop, or tilling the ground.

The learned and the wise, the noble of birth—
All ranks and conditions of men upon earth—
Improve well your time, your duties perform,
In youth or in age, through sunshine or storm.

Then press bravely on in the path that is right,
Your thoughts, and your words and actions, keep bright ;
Ever turn something up, don't wait for the tide,
Be faithful, keep true, and loving abide.

"THEY SAY."

How oft' the sons of Adam's race
Their neighbour's business try to trace ;
The daughters, too, of mother Eve
Will sometimes cause you to believe
Their friends are scarcely kind or fair,
And in their dealings not quite square ;
But both the men and maidens gay
Should keep a watch on what "they say."

THEY SAY—*continued*.

"They say" is open to abuse,
And sometimes is a lame excuse,
Behind their back to say of friends
What does not to their honour tend ;
They hint, in language rather strong,
Their neighbour's purse is not too long,
In fact, they scarce can pay their way,
Is what these busy bodies say.

Another has his purse well filled,
Yet, sad to say, is not well willed,
He hoards his silver and his gold,
And will not part with it, we're told ;
Though some good cause is needing "brass,"
He will not give them much, alas !
Talkers, he may be one of those,
Who sounds no trumpet where he goes.

The talkers yet have quite a store
Of news to tell, they gab things o'er :
When so-and-so were at the town,
They bought a span new hat, or gown,
They think it fits them slack or tight,
The stuff is heavy, or it's light,
It does not suit them well, "they say" ;
The busy bodies talk away.

The farmers also get their share
Said of them—sometimes hardly fair :
They fear they've mixed the "old black cow"
Along with white, pure milk, ere now ;
Or when the cheese the farmers make,
They to the market butter take,
Their eggs are either white or small.
The weeds, alas, are rank and tall.

Shopkeepers, too, "they say" talk o'er :
They do not much admire their store,
Say they, it is not up-to-date,
Closing too early or too late ;

THEY SAY—*continued.*

They fear they'll go against the wall,
Some goods they do not keep at all,
Then show to them a better way,
Is our advice to what "they say."

The merchants, while they buy and sell,
Their own nests mind to feather well :
"They say" : although they l uy poor stuff,
They advertise and make a puff —
Although their goods are second-rate,
Look out! they like to sell first-rate :
Or stock below the mark, they say
They push it on and make it pay.

The folk who woo and wed, maybe,
"They say," will talk of pretty free,
Of course, they don't approve the match
The parties will not have much "catch" :
Or, they may find it out too late
They should have kept a single state.
It seems too bad they thus should talk,
For married life they'd like to walk.

Let each one guard the little tongue,
Don't let it say one thing that's wrong :
Repeat the kind words o'er again,
Both boys and girls, women and men :
The tongue unruly, let it be
Restrained by grace so rich and free ;
Let's do our duty, pay our way,
Whatever talkers do or say.

———

A CHRISTIAN GENTLEMAN.

Could a man inherit Samson's strength,
With Og, the king of Basham's length :
Or fill the giant's armour who
The youthful David did o'erthrow.

45

A CHRISTIAN GENTLEMAN—*continued.*

Could he secure the noted fame
Of him to whom queen Candace came ;
His cattle numerous as Job's of Uz,
And corn fields rich as those of Boaz ;

The learning which Gamalial had,
With stores of knowledge, good and bad ;
Or, coming to our land and times,
Possess wide tracts of fertile soils ;

Or streets of building grand and tall,
And lakes of water, great and small,
His coaches and his horses be
A splendid turnout—nice to see ;

His dress of faultless fit and style,
Which well becomes his rank and times ;
His ancestry traced past the name
Of John, of Magna Charter fame ;

Of gold and silver a rich store,
And still increasing more and more,
His ships of merchandise let land
With gems from many a foreign strand.

Let titles, honours, crowd him fast,
And earthly friendships, while they last ;
Still multiply, and add to these
A crown and empire, if you please.

Be these united : strength and length,
Together with his fame and wealth,
However useful these may be,
Rich fertile land and ships at sea ;

His outward conduct free from blame,
His moral character the same ;
Yet something's lacking ere we can
Call him a Christian gentleman.

A CHRISTIAN GENTLEMAN —*continued*.

That something is true faith in Christ,
Who is the Way, the Truth, and Life ;
Firm confidence in Him alone,
Who did for guilty man atone :

Becomes a branch of the true Vine,
Who was both human and Divine,
And proving by his outward fruit
That Jesus is the living root.

By words and actions—gentle, kind,
Show forth a pure and loving mind,
Still pressing on the heavenly race,
Supported by a Saviour's grace :

Then, whatever titles he
May have, or which may lacking be,
Assured we may, and truly can,
Say—" there's a Christian gentleman."

MERRY LITTLE LARK.

Well done merry little lark,
    With thy music sweet and gay,
Singing thy Creator's praise
    On a sunny April day.

Up and up, ascending higher,
    Singing as thou wings't thy flight,
Warbling forth thy choicest lyre,
    In the lovely morning light.

Like a maiden, pure and fair,
    Singing in her fresh young glee,
Trusting in the loving care
    Which preserves both her and thee.

47

Or a youth who at his work
  Singing in his early prime,
Brooding not o'er doubts and fears,
  In God's praise employs his time.

Boys and girls, maidens and men,
  Well may each example take,
Those who are husbands with their wives
  Unto heaven sweet music make.

Sound through earth and sea's and air
  Mighty music loud yet sweet,
Praising Jesus, wonderous fair,
  Him in hearty homage greet.

Like the merry little lark,
  With its music blithe and gay,
May we sing God's praises here,
  And thorugh everlasting day.

Up and up ascending higher,
  Till within the pearly gate,
May we strike the golden lyre,
  Saints and angels emulate.

EXAMPLE.

Should we throw a tiny pebble
  Into waters deep and wide,
How it waves it o'er and ripples
  Till it reach from side to side.

If you listen to the echo,
  When you shout or sing away
Joining in as if in chorus
  Sounding back again away.

EXAMPLE—*continued.*

See we now a cawing crow light
    On the newly covered seed,
Soon a host of black companions
    Also light to take a feed.

When a sheep has leapt right over
    Into pastures fresh and sweet,
Soon we notice many others
    Are inclined to take a treat.

When a cow chooses to ramble
    Gets into a field of corn,
Soon the others its example
    Follow after hoof and horn.

Think we now of youthful horses
    Grazing on the mountain side,
One runs down in sprightly gallop,
    Soon the others after glide.

Notice now, ascending higher,
    Little children at their play.
Listen to their childhood's prattle,
    Copy of what others say.

Still observe them, when they walk
    Place their feet where father trod,
But for steps so very long,
    They may have to hop and nod.

Then again when boys and girls
    Say harsh words or give cross looks,
Others give back looks and words
    Which are better out of books.

Give kind loving words and actions
    To your friends where'er you meet,
They will follow your example
    And with hearty welcome greet.

EXAMPLE—*continued*,

Thus we see the vast importance
  Of example pure and good
When we think that from each other,
  Each one draws much moral food.

How we've often read with pleasure
  Of the saints of other days,
And been cheered by their example
  To press on in Christian ways.

But by far the best example
  Of our own or any age
Is our Saviour of whose history
  We have read on sacred page.

He's a true and faithful copy,
  Free from blemish sin or stain,
Who came down from highest heaven
  Sinners to win back again.

THE BOYS WHO ARE WANTED.

What class of boys are wanted now
  To make our country strong?
Boys who will do their duty well
  And shun the path that's wrong.

Boys who are trusty and will work,
  And strictly honest be ;
Who'll act the same when master's out
  As when he's there to see.

If country life should be his lot,
  And farming be his trade,
We hope he's active with his tools—
  His scraper, fork, and spade.

THE BOYS WHO ARE WANTED—*continued.*

At morn and evening, milking time,
    Be sure and milk them clean ;
Pure milk's a beverage, rich and good,
    For peasant or for queen.

If smith or wheelwright he should be,
    Right well his hammer use ;
Just hit the nail upon the head
    As quickly as you choose.

Avoid the village public-house —
    Firm, staunch abstainers be :
So use your leisure hours that you
    May some improvement see.

Boys, who if they reside in town
    And have to wait in shops,
Will show the goods quite pleasantly
    Whoever in doth pop.

And even if the goods don't suit.
    When they have looked them o'er,
Still show a cheerful countenance
    As if they'd bought a score.

Boys, who whate'er their business be,
    Don't grumble and repine,
Who are good tempered all day long,
    And well improve their time.

Boys who avoid the pipe and glass
    And everything that's wrong,
And live a truly Christian life—
    Such make their country strong.

Boys such as these, where'er they dwell —
    In country, village, town,
Will be a credit to their home
    And well deserve renown.

THE BOYS WHO ARE WANTED—*continued.*

So when these boys have grown to men,
    And really need a wife,
We think they'll make some loving girls
    True husbands, good for life.

———

THE GIRLS WHO ARE WANTED.

What kind of girls are wanted now
    To make our home-life bright :
Girls who are good—sweet tempered
    From morning until night.

Girls who are truthful and modest,
    Aspiring to that which is right,
Ne'er trying to shun a plain duty,
    Who lofty or low will not slight.

Girls who are careful and saving,
    Yet generous to a good cause,
And whilst cheering our home with sweet music,
    Yet knowing full well when to pause.

Girls who can wash, clean, or mangle,
    Or play with the children at times ;
Can make them a good dose of toffy,
    But always abstain from the wines.

The girls who honour their parents
    As they quickly advance in life,
Are the girls who if they get married
    Will make kind mothers and wives.

'Tis they who at their own fireside
    Will bright and pleasant be,
Who are kind and gentle at home
    When strangers do not see.

52

THE GIRLS WHO ARE WANTED—*continued*.

Who have a smile and loving word
    For those with whom they dwell,
Who by their daily conduct prove
    They love their home folks well.

Girls who can make or mend a dress,
    Or sew the buttons on ;
Can knit or darn the stockings when
    The feet are almost gone.

Girls who can cook a dinner well,
    Make pastry if you please ;
Can tempt a patient's appetite,
    When they are not at ease.

Girls who have some good common sense,
    Whom fashions can't deceive,
While dressing prim and well and neat
    Can what is needless leave.

Girls such as prove their wisdom too
    In what they do or say,
Who lovingly and kindly
    Drive wrath and strife away.

Girls who like ancient Martha
    Can household duties take ;
But like her sister Mary
    The best of choices make.

The girls who trust and honour
    The Saviour of mankind,
Who in His loving service
    Their choicest pleasures find.

These are the girls now wanted
    To guide each nations' homes,
As sisters, wives and mothers,
    From cottage up to thrones.

A CHEERFUL CUP OF TEA.

Tune: *Auld Lang Syne.*

We'll not forget our old-time friends,
    With whom we used to play;
We'll not forget our childhood's mates,
    Though they are far away.

CHORUS.

And when we meet we'll con things o'er,
    How old times used to be,
And pledge old friendships once again
    In cups of cheerful tea.

For this we hope will do no harm,
    Nor cause our heads to ache,
And when we travel home again
    It won't affect our gait.

CHORUS.

And when we meet, &c.

At times we played at tick awhile,
    And then said "barly" out;
Anon, upon the old barn floor
    The marbles bounced about.

CHORUS.

And when we meet, &c.

Sometimes we jumped a little rill
    Across from shore to shore,
Or fished within the waters, which
    Rushed onward as before.

CHORUS.

And when we meet, &c.

Again, across the fields we roamed,
    Or gathered sweet wild flowers,
And looked the hedge for birdie's nest
    Full many a youthful hour.

CHORUS.
And when we meet, &c.

In havest time we worked among
The fresh, new, fragrant hay,
Or listened to the lark's glad song,
Almost as blithe as they.

CHORUS.
And when we meet, &c.

In school-days we had chosen mates,
When learning A B C ;
Since then a score of years have passed,
Or may be two or three.

CHORUS.
And when we meet, &c.

In towns and country don't forget
The days of bonny yore,
And still be true to present friends,
And prize them more and more.

CHORUS.
So old and new and future friends,
Though rich or poor you be,
Let's pledge again your health and wealth
In cheerful, pleasant tea.

GOOD MORNING.

Good morning, children at your play,
Come kindly tell your age to-day ;
Is it four, five, six, or some more—
How far below just half-a-score ?
Your age to be both kind and true,
In all you think or say or do ;
Obey your parents, come to Him
Who came to save you from your sin.

GOOD MORNING—*continued.*

Good morning maidens, let me say,
Some nearing two half-scores to-day :
Whilst hoping you are prim and neat,
From bonnet downwards to your feet,
We hope you also are inclined
To cultivate a noble mind,
And if you think of being wed,
Just look before you leap 'tis said.

Good morn, young men, how old are you ?—
Nineteen, twenty, or twenty-two.
We hope you've a good aim in life,
And mean to conquer in the strife :
Abstain from all that's base and vain,
And from the right way never wane,
And when you're tired of single life
Select a truly Christian wife.

Good day to wives and husbands too,
Some thirty, forty, fifty you ;
Though you have steered so far from port,
We hope you still each other court—
In love and peace together live,
And each to each due honour give—
Both faithful, trusting Christ our King,
Enjoy sweet peace beneath His wing.

Good evening, friends advanced in years,
Still soar above your doubts and fears ;
Take courage—press towards the shore—
Look up, 'tis better on before.
The race still run with patience look
To Jesus, who says in the Book—
Be faithful unto death and He
A crown of life will give to thee.

A TRIP TO MANCHESTER.

The Manchester City is nice to behold,
For those who have leisure, brass, silver and gold ;
Our friends who to purchase have means and the will,
May do so with pleasure in shops or Shudehill.

Great city, so famous for cotton and wealth,
Long still be continued good commerce and health ;
Manufacturing people in labour abound,
Fair business and profits still flourish all round.

From Staffordshire, Cheshire and Midlands they slip,
To Manchester City speed off for a trip ;
Vast multitudes travelled a short time ago,
The city to view, and also the show.

The Royal was excellent—horses and cows—
Variety splendid, with implements, ploughs,
If properly worked to till well the ground,
For miles in a circle the show-yard around.

The City's attractions are easily found—
To the right or the left and forward abound—
Cathedral and chapels and churches view o'er,
Grand Gospel accept and prize more and more.

Town Hall and the Royal Exchange also see,
Ornamental and useful there meet and agree ;
Art Gallery and parks' fair beauties behold,
Free Library's stores of knowledge unfold.

Belle Vue has its laurels, what multitudes go
And visit its gardens, perchance have a row ;
The apes and the birds, wild animals too,
Inspection deserve to nature so true.

Be mindful all, please, and keep to the right,
Avoiding all wrong e'er walk in the light :
When out or returning before after trip,
Pure virtue and honour ne'er lose or let slip.

THE WHEELWRIGHT.

Hard by the country turnpike
.The wheelwright's shop doth stand,
And he the farmer's woodwork
Most chiefly doth command.

He has his timber drying
Convenient in his yard ;
In lofty piles it reareth
Till it is firm and hard.

He is a proper workman
And uses well his plane—
His axe, his saw, his chisel
Has not long idle lain.

He makes the farmer's waggons
From bottom to top wraith,
Or mends his cart and trap wheels
With felloes, spokes and nave.

But when too old for mending,
Span new wheels he will make,
With body, shafts and top-gear,
And for down hill a brake.

He knows well how to fix them
Just right for whizzing round :
With horses to assist them
They quickly clear the ground.

And well he does his duty
From morning until night,
When he retires from business
Until the morning light.

And when the week is ended,
He joins on Sabbath day
To worship in God's temple,
And hear of Christ the way.

THE WHEELWRIGHT—*continued.*

When Sabbath rest is over,
　　And Monday morn comes round,
He has not left his conscience
　　Upon the temple ground.

While diligent in business,
　　Heeding the sacred word ;
Still fervent in the spirit,
　　Serving his faithful Lord.

Then as our time is speeding
　　Swifter than swiftest wheels,
May each one now improve it,
　　As onward fast it steals.

CUCKOO.

Come cuckoo, harbinger of spring,
We love to hear thee shout and sing ;
Thy joyous note it seems to cheer,
Though dull or bright the atmosphere.

Thou singest on the mountain top,
Or o'er where rushing waters sop
Amidst the forest in the trees,
High o'er the notes of humming bees.

Above the verdant green hill side,
Or valley where sweet flowers reside ;
Sometimes cuckooing near at hand,
At others far above the land.

With joy we heard in days of yore,
When we were young, just three or four !
Thee shouting cuckoo in spring days,
And tried to imitate thy lays.

CUCKOO—*continued.*

Since then long years have sped and gone,
But still thy tune is the same one ;
Yet though we've heard it o'er and o'er,
It charms us as in days of yore.

Haste cuckoo, messenger of spring,
We love to hear thee shout and sing ;
Thy pleasant note of tuneful cheer
We gladly welcome year by year.

CONTENTMENT.

The Apostle Paul writes : I have learned, in
whatsoever state I am, therewith to be content.
But godliness, with contentment, is great
gain.

If mother Eve had been content,
With what our Heavenly Father sent :
Ripe, sweet, rich fruit, with plum and cherry,
She with Adam had been merry.

But, sad to say, they both did eat
What was not meant for human meat :
They disobeyed God's good command,
Their Eden lost—and till'd the land.

If the wise king had been content
His wisdom in God's service spent
His glory would have brighter beamed,
If vanity he had not gleaned.

Saint Paul, a many trials had—
Some thought him good and others bad—
Still he had learned to be content,
As on in duty's path he went.

He gloried in the Cross of Christ,
And never was ashamed to hoist
The signal of his banner high,
Whose name still charms both earth and sky.

Each may from Christ contentment gain,
A happiness which will not wane :
Come as directed in God's book—
Confess, repent, believe and look.

Come high and low, both rich and poor,
And gain contentment from this store ;
Fruits of the Spirit bear and yield
Along the Gospel harvest field.

Each onward march and do not stop,
The kind words say, the good seed drop,
And let contentment deck and grace
A loving heart and smiling face.

THE BEST GIFT.

Away out in the sunny east,
  A lady once did dwell ;
Three sons she had, each one no doubt
  The mother loved full well.

So ere she went away awhile,
  A journey long to take :
They each in token of their love,
  Did her a present make.

One gave a marble tablet with
  The inscription of her name :
Upon its placid surface there
  Showed forth the letters plain.

THE BEST GIFT—*continued.*

The second he presented her
    With fragrant flowers so gay,
As sweet and pure as those we see
    In merry month of May.

The third one to his mother came,
    And in effect did say—
I've brought no tablet of great fame,
    No fragrant sweet nosegay.

But I've a heart and here your name
    Inscribed shall ever be :
Your memory kind mother dear
    Shall precious be to me.

Full of affection shall this heart
    Follow where'er you go ;
And where you take repose and rest,
    My heart will stay also.

We scarcely need to say which gift
    Would far the dearest be ;
We know the mother most would prize
    The gift of number three.

'Tis yet the same the wide world o'er,
    With those who're one in heart ;
When meeting or when parting how
    The tear drop oft will start.

Still parents, brothers, sisters, prize
    The affections of the heart
More highly than the tablet grand
    Or fragrant flowers so smart.

The youth who fain would gain a miss,
    If he can win her heart ;
We hope he will not do amiss :
    He's made a cheering start.

THE BEST GIFT—*continued.*

Vice versa too let it be said,
   If she has gained his heart ;
And each thus mutually agree,
   'Twould be unwise to part.

And when the wedding day arrives,
   And she becomes his bride,
O may they join both heart and hand,
   To travel side by side.

Most most important too for each
   To choose the better part :
To listen to the Father's voice,
   Saying— give me thy heart.

Let each comply with this request,
   And trust our Saviour dear :
Sweet comfort, grace, and peace and rest,
   He'll bless you with and cheer.

A. B, C.

A, B, C, D, E, F, G,
Let us now consider thee :
Little children can you tell
Which is M and which is L ?
When you come to O, P, Q,
O's and Q's are nice for you,
Though one shape, you may find out,
Q has a tail, and O's without.

Now, just think of R, S, T,
Someone spell them along with E.
Teacher, please, grant our request—
Give we little folks some rest ?
For a mixture work and play,
We rather like from day to day.
When you repeat the A, B, C,
Let them each well learned be.

When you arrive at X, Y, Z,
Let them be well said and read ;
On your youthful memory fix,
Each and all of the twenty-six.
Princes and peasants alike must try
To learn from A to Z and Y ;
All who've attained to wise D.D.,
Once began with A, B, C.

THE PRINCIPAL THING.

Some boys and girls at school or home,
Whatever else may go or come,
Their chief desires are toys and play:
" Bother the lessons," so they say.

Others more wisely act by far,
Pushing the perseverance car :
Their lessons they will learn, or try,
At play or work, press on---not cry.

Some youthful men and maidens gay,
We fear are vain from day to day :
Their coats and dresses, bonnets, hats,
And of their beaus they're thinking at.

Anon when—settled down in life
As married husband, wedded wife :
How anxious next to feather well—
A nest, and so in comfort dwell.

If farmers, of their crops they boast,
Their cattle, young and old a host ;
Prizing too highly things down here,
Forgetting scripture themes we fear.

64

THE PRINCIPAL THING--*continued*.

Some merchants, eager to get rich,
They scarcely seem to care a vetch
Whether their trade is wrong or right
If they are gaining silver bright.

Some lawyers seem to plead a cause—
If good or bad—without a pause ;
Though falsehoods or the truth is told,
There chief desire to gain some gold.

The miser's chief desire is money,
Though cloudy be the sky or sunny—
For this he strives, for this he craves,
His wealth he treasures up and saves.

The drunkard's one desire, alas !
Is quaffing liquor from the glass :
Drinking until he falls at length,
O'erthrown by its poor paltry strength.

Others again desire their name
Enrolled upon the scroll of fame :
But human titles don't long last,
For time and tide are rushing past.

Others again a mighty host
Of Jesus' righteousness they boast ;
Walking in wisdom's pleasant way,
True pleasure have from day to day.

May each whate'er their rank or grade,
Every profession, every trade :
Their duties, numerous or few,
Still let all cheerfully pursue.

The principal true wisdom find
Comfort and joy, and peace of mind ;
The chief desire, great end and aim,
The one thing needful to attain.

THE SHOEMAKER.

In country and in village,
  In towns you often see
The cobbler in his workshop—
  A useful man is he.

It adds much to your comfort
  To have shoes to your feet,
Though feet were made before them,
  Still good shoes are a treat.

Quite pleasantly he'll measure
  You for a pair of boots ;
And we admit with pleasure
  They much improve your looks.

He kens about the leather,
  He cuts and hammers well ;
All seasons and all weather,
  He'll make good boots or sell.

Right well he plies his wax-ends,
  When he has used his awl :
Oft you see him pull and bend,
  When at his shop you call.

Then if your boots want soling,
  Or if they want new heels :
The cobbler is condoling,
  E'en to the tips and steels.

Three cheers for honest workmen,
  Though working for the feet :
Still make good shoes for boys and men
  Turning them out quite neat.

Each maker and each wearer
  Be wise and don't delay ;
All choose the path of wisdom,
  The happy Christian way.

THE SHOEMAKER—*continued*.

Shod with the preparation
   Of gospel, peace and joy;
Your talents and your leisure
   In doing good employ.

———

MACCLESFIELD MARKET DAY.

Hail! borough town of Macclesfield,
We thee a hearty greeting yield;
Still may prosperity and wealth
United be with rosy health.

Healthy in body, spirit, mind,
Still may thy sons and daughters find
Pure wisdom's bright and pleasant ways;
Cheerful and happy be their days.

Thy market day is still renowned,
The farmers come from miles around;
Clough Forest, Wincle and Langley,
From Presbury and Alderley.

From many a hill and country side,
Some walk, and others swiftly ride:
Their cheese and butter—eggs as well,
To Macclesfield they bring and sell.

The shops are decked in bright array,
Material, clothing—useful, gay,
The farmers from the hills and flats
May here rig out with coats and hats.

For town and country ladies round
New garments also here abound,
Some medium, others chaste and neat,
Capes, bonnets, hats, shoes for the feet,

Pure groceries, choice coffees, tea,
Good flavour and pure blends there be ;
Provisions sweet, substantial, pure,
Which should good customers secure.

Macclesfield papers read and see
News, information, there will be
Adieu, at present, Macclesfield,
Some further muse we hope to yield.

THE WAY TO SUCCESS.

From all that's wrong turn round about,
Right in the Scripture way set out ;
Whoe'er may tempt, turn not aside,
Abstain from evil, stem the tide.

To watch and pray at once begin,
And parley not with any sin :
Accept the grace so freely given,
To help us on our way to heaven.

Of course we each must persevere
Through thick or thin, o'ercast or clear—
Waiting for neither chance or luck—
Press bravely on with zeal and pluck.

In literature would we succeed,
Each study persevere and read ;
However learned the scholar be,
He climbed aloft from A B C.

Would we succeed in science arts,
Though small and feeble be the start ;
Yet perseverance day by day
Begins at length to make headway.

THE WAY TO SUCCESS—*continued.*

The florist—if he would succeed—
Must learn to sow, and plant, and weed ;
The husbandman garners his crop,
Ere yet the rip'n'd grain doth drop.

In business if we would succeed,
Details attend with steady speed ;
Our duty honestly pursue—
With numerous customers, or few.

The heights successful men have gained,
Were not by indolence attained ;
They laboured on from day to day,
And persevered in duty's way.

As Christian workers to succeed,
We must Christ's merits trust and plead ;
Be clothed in Jesu's righteousness,
Pure, spotless, all sufficient dress.

Our talents one, two, five or ten
Improve as faithful husbandmen ;
The good seed scatter left and right,
Till harvest ripens rich and bright.

To be successful—persevere,
Cheerful upon the right way steer,
Where duty calls each march along,
'Till victory crowns our triumph song.

YOU SEE AND WE THINK.

The boy who his lessons will cabbage or shirk,
Or get others to do him his personal work,
Whatever his station or talents may be,
He will not get high as a scholar you see ;
But if, while yet young, he honestly learns,
And does not to shirking or trifling turn,
He'll either attain or get near the brink
Of eminent scholarship—so we should think.

YOU SEE AND WE THINK —*continued.*

If a boy at his work lightly over it skip,
His time or his master's lets unimproved slip ;
Whatever his strength or his business may be,
He wont make a very good workman you see.
But when a boy buckles to work with a will,
And does his work neatly, and does it with skill,
If making a waggon or wielding a link
He'll make something out as a workman we think.

If puffing a pipe or perchance a cigar,
He enters the public and drinks at the bar,
Emerging outside loaded crooked maybe,
He's on the down-grade rather fast don't you see.
But let him avoid and shun puffing a cloud,
And avoid bad companions, both noisy and loud ;
Go on the right pathway—abstain from the drink—
A promising youngster is he we should think.

The young man when wooing or courting a lass,
Just gains her affections then leaves her—alas !
Without a good reason, whoe'er he may be,
Young maidens with wisdom will shun him you see.
The young man who considers things carefully o'er,
Who looks well —not flirting or leaping before ;
Other things being right, then please do not shrink,
He should make a loving, good husband we think.

When husbands and wives often grumble and fret,
And frown at each other or get in a pet ;
Though dwelling in cottage, or mansion may be,
They're lacking in love and comfort you see ;
But when they each bear and forbear too in love,
Both loving and serving one Master above,
And pulling together, in unity's link,
They have pleasure as husband and wife we should think.

The farmer or tradesman who makes short of weight,
Not doing to others the thing that is right ;
However attentive to business he be,
He isn't as good as he should be you see.

YOU SEE AND WE THINK—*continued.*

But those who give fair, honest measure and weight,
Can manage to look in your face pretty straight ;
At dealings unfair these men do not wink —
Square, upright and honest in business we think.

People sitting bolt upright in pew or in chair,
And listlessly gazing about during prayer ;
Though learned or illiterate these people may be,
They seem sadly wanting in reverence you see.
Let each bow in reverence, and each take a part
And render to Jesus true homage of heart ;
Then turn not aside should evil allure—
Press onward and Christward, and upward be sure.

KIND WORDS AND LOOKS.

The kind words, all speak them, repeat them oft o'er
In every land, nation, climate and shore ;
Never needlessly tread upon people's corns—
Pass by, or skip over the pricks and the thorns.

Avoid all the gruff words—unkind or unfair—
All shirk them and leave them, don't let them ensnare :
Just give them no quarter, but leave them unsaid,
Speak gently and lovingly, kindly, instead.

The kind words don't rankle, they blister no tongues,
Then speak them and read them, in prose and in song,
They help to encourage and cheer people on,
So bid all unchristian, unkind words begone.

Kind looks, how they cheer us and help us along,
In country, in village, or 'midst city's throng :
Then give all the gladness and sunshine you can,
To boys or to girls, to women or men.

Avoid all the harsh looks, forsake all the frowns,
In every homestead, in country or towns ;
Don't give them or look them, but bid them begone,
The kind looks and smiles are better.   Well done !

Kind actions, the fruits of kind words and bright looks,
Don't shirk or neglect, or discard from your books ;
Each do unto others as you'd be done by,
Thus easing their burden, their griefs, or their sigh.

Abstain from all acts which cause sorrow or pain,
Pursue the right pathway, through loss or through gain ;
Seek peace, love and concord wherever you be,
At home or abroad, on land or the sea.

Kind words, looks and actions, let all patronise,
The high and the lowly, the simple and wise ;
Please kindly don't tread, or stamp on our corns,
Pass by, and skip over all pricks and all thorns.

LOVE ONE ANOTHER.

*" A new Commandment I give unto you :
that ye love one another."*

Let all obey Jesu's command—
Saints of all sects — of every land—
Who prostrate at his footstool fall
Trusting in Christ their all in all.

Who take the scriptures for their guide,
And chart through life, whate'er betide;
Let all Christ's armies march along
United rout all sin and wrong.

Like Bishop Ryle and Garrat make
Some sacrifice for Jesu's sake:
Encouraging each other on
Let bigotry now all begone.

LOVE ONE ANOTHER—*continued.*

Let Wesleyan president now take
Archbishop's hand in loving shake :
Each true and loyal ever stand,
Obeying still this new command.

While Presbyterians firm or free
Should cordially as one agree ;
Accounting minor things as dross,
Each pointing sinners to the cross.

Now let the Christians called " Baptists "
Unite with Congregationalists :
Let dipped and sprinkled trust in Him
Whose blood alone can cleanse from sin.

Primitives and New Connexionists,
Each be enrolled amongst the list
Of those of every tribe and land,
Owning and loving Christ's command.

The friends in grey and broad-brimmed hat
Meet Christian army on this flat,
Work for one captain— nobly stand,
Obeying Jesu's great command.

Lay preachers, scripture readers, meet
Before one common mercy seat ;
Clergy and Christian people find
In Christ pure joy and peace of mind.

Christians of every land and clime,
Christ's faithful followers, all combine
Shoulder to shoulder march along
Against the hosts of sin and wrong.

Who trust in Jesus —Christ our Lord,
And for their guide take His own word.
Act each to each as friend and brother,
Obey Christ's word " Love one another."

73

HEAVEN.

"Who are these, and whence came they?"

Musing of Heaven bright and fair,
And of the Saints safe landed there ;
Through Christ alone the only way,
They reached the home of perfect day.

Peter and James and John are there,
Andrew with Luke and Matthew share
Mansions of rest before the throne,
Through Christ who did for sin atone.

Barnabas and Paul contend no more
On that serene and peaceful shore ;
Vibrates up there no jarring string,
In sweetest harmony they sing.

The Christian Fathers toils are o'er,
They hunger now and thirst no more :
There persecutions never come
To New Jerusalem—dear home.

Confessors, Martyrs—noble host
Of Jesus only still they boast ;
On earth they bore His cross and shame,
Rejoicing in their Saviour's name.

But now their warfare all is past,
The joys of Heaven always last :
Waiving their palms before the throne,
Victory ascribe to Christ alone.

Great Preachers of the Gospel word,
Who loved and served one common Lord :
Some loved the Church, and some dissent,
Their talents for their Saviour spent.

On minor points they differed here,
But there these small points disappear ;
Which Christian sect they helped along,
Is not their theme, is not their song.

HEAVEN—*continued.*

United now before the throne,
Their theme is Christ and Him alone ;
The Authors of our Sacred Songs
To various Christian sects belonged.

Methinks in Heaven they now agree,
Together praise the Lamb with glee—
Bernard, with Watts and Toplady,
Zinzendorf, Wesleys, and Brady.

Peronet, Olivers, and Heber,
In the Lamb's bright hall with Boner—
Let them join with hosts of others
Of Christ's true friends and followers.

If clothed in Jesu's righteousness,
On earth Christ's faithful witnesses ;
Whate'er their sect, or name or tongue,
Join in the new triumphant song.

If thus in Heaven the Saints agree
Where all is radiant, fair and free ;
Whilst musing thus it seems quite clear,
Christians should love each other here.

HYMN.

Tune—*City of the Jasper Walls.*

O Heaven above, where all is light
  No darkness ever comes :
Where ne'er appears no shades of night
  In that eternal home.
No need of sun, or moon, or stars,
  For Jesus is its light ;
No need of earthly garments there.
  For all are robed in white.

HYMN—*continued.*

CHORUS.

O home above, O home so bright,
No need of sun, or moon, or stars,
O home for ever bright.

O Heaven, so fair, where all is pure,
Where comes no taint of sin ;
But sinners washed in Jesu's blood
Shall freely enter in,
For Jesus came down from above
To make an end of sin,
And died on Calvary's Cross for us
Eternal life to win.

CHORUS.

O home, so fair : O home, so pure,
Where sinners washed in Jesu's blood,
May freely enter in.

O heaven, so calm, where all is peace,
No strife or din of war ;
No pen can paint these bowers of ease,
So grand its mansions are ;
O may we run the Christian race,
" 'Tis better on before " ;
And through rich, free, unbounded grace,
Enter through Heaven's door.

CHORUS.

O home, so calm ; O home of peace,
O may we gain those bowers of ease
Through Christ alone, the door.

O Heaven of joy, of peace, of love,
Which Jesus died to win ;
Our highest notes, in Heaven above,
We'll gladly raise to Him ;

HYMN—*continued.*

And when life's pilgrimage is past,
And Jordan rolls before,
May we through Jesu's merits gain
Fair Canaan's peaceful shore.

CHORUS.

O home of joy, O home of love,
Half of thy glory ne'er was told
Jerusalem above.

THE WAY TO HEAVEN.

Tune—*The Better Land.*

Kind teacher, tell me how to find
The way to the land of the undefiled:
I perceive by reading the Scripture lore,
No sin is found on the heavenly shore,
And all sorrow is banished for evermore.
They need not the light of the sun by day,
The Lamb, the Lamb, the Lamb's its light.

If I climb morality's top most height,
And form my conduct by the law most straight,
And do unto others the thing that is right,
In word, in thought, and in deed upright,
Ever keeping my character pure and bright,
Is this the way to that Heaven of light?
Still short, still short, still short, my boy!

Or through the Saints, who in olden days
Acknowledged Jehovah in all their ways:
And from Him derived strength and grace to stand
The fiery trials from the enemies hand.
May I come through those who the Martyr's fate
Most firmly suffered for the Saviour's sake?
Not so, not so, not so, my boy.

The way is plain in the sacred book,
Simply turn and repent, believe, and look
On Jesus, who suffered on Calvary's Cross
To bless and to save the world that was lost.
Through trusting alone in the Saviour you'll find
The way to the home of the undefiled—
Through Christ, through Christ, through Christ,
    alone.

HYMN OF PRAISE.

Tune—*Mile's Lane*.

Hail! Father, God, Thy name we praise,
  We laud and bless our King :
Who to Thy flock in time of need,
  Dost ever succour bring.

When we were wandering far from Thee,
  In barren paths of sin ;
Thou did'st devise a way whereby
  Our precious souls to win.

Thy love to us was rich and free,
  Unmeasured, unconfined ;
Thou gav'st Thy well beloved Son,
  A ransom for mankind.

Hail! Jesus, Saviour, of our race,
  Who came from Heaven above :
The shining ranks of Angels left
  So vast, so free, Thy love.

Thou did'st a full atonement make
  On Calvary's rugged tree ;
Our sins and guilt did'st bear and take,
  To set the sinner free.

HYMN OF PRAISE—*continued*.

Blest Holy Spirit, each convince,
  Give us to feel our need ;
And guide the wanderer to the fold
  Where Christ His flock doth feed.

Hail ! Triune Deity adored,
  We magnify Thy name ;
And hope to cast our crowns before
  The throne that will not wane.

———

*" Come unto Me all ye that labour, and are
heavy laden, and I will give you rest."*—Matt.,
c. 11, v. 28.

Dost thou feel thy sins a burden,
  Heavy upon thee ?
" Cast thy burden," saith the Saviour,
  " Upon Me."

I, who have so long been captive
  In the chains of sin,
Can I yet to peace and freedom
  Enter in ?

Can I come so sinful, guilty,
  To be cleansed from sin ?
Will the precious blood of Jesus
  Pardon win ?

He has opened wide a fountain,
  May I lave therein ?
Will it make me—vile and sinful—
  Pure within ?

If I come through Jesus only—
  Simply trust in him,
He will welcome, pardon, cleanse me
  From my sin.

79

HYMN –*continued.*

God so loved a world of sinners
  That His son He gave,
And whoever trusteth in Him
  Life shall have.

And if faithful through life's journey,
  Pressing towards the mark,
He will not forsake or leave thee
  In the dark.

Singing on the brink of Jordan,
  Clinging unto Him,
Through the precious blood of Jesus
  Victory win.

And when passing through the river,
  Thou need'st fear no ill,
For the waters shall be shallow,
  At His Will.

Then when landed safely over
  On fair Canaan's shore,
Sing the song of Him who loved thee
  Evermore.

CHARITY.

We ask not which denomination
Of the Christian Church you own ;
Do we build on one foundation,
Christ, the Living Corner Stone.

Jesu's righteousness and merit,
Our one all sufficient plea :
For us each He made atonement,
When He died on Calvary.

CHARITY—*continued.*

And we take the sacred Scriptures,
As our guide-chart of the way ;
Through our pilgrimage and journey,
To the home of brighter day.

On this wide, broad Christian basis,
We can each as brethren meet,
Lay our small and minor difference,
At our loving Saviour's feet.

Let us not waste ammunition,
On our friends along the line ;
There are hosts of sin to conquer,
Which should occupy our time.

Let us march a mighty army,
Still of various ranks along,
Owning Christ our one great captain,
Till we shout the victor's song.

So may each Denomination
Build on Jesus Christ alone ;
Rest on Him, sure. true foundation—
Rock of Ages—Corner Stone.

THE MINISTER'S LONG COURTSHIP.

In the days of slow stage coaches,
The good old times long past
Before railways or motor cars,
Things did not speed so fast.

A minister, whose name was John,
Good quiet man was he :
He saw and loved a maiden fair,
A modest girl was she.

THE MINISTER'S LONG COURTSHIP—*continued.*

Their love was calm and patient,
　Not rushing like the wind ;
And yet it was not transient,
　It was a lasting kind.

True love grew into courtship,
　As fruit from blossoms grow ;
Yet patiently they waited
　Like husbandmen who sow.

His Reverence somewhat bashful,
　The courtship was not fast ;
They'd made but little progress
　For six-and-a-half years past.

Progress, however, must be made,
　One day as oft before,
In solemn silence they had sat
　Awhile, but it past o'er.

He mustered courage to enquire
　If he might take a kiss ?
He'd waited 'ull six years or more,
　One would not be amiss.

"Just as you like," the maiden said,
　" Only be becoming " ;
So when they duly were prepared,
　The sweet one was forthcoming.

So after this a short six months
　Did quickly pass away :
Affection was not fickle, to
　Seven years in courtship stay.

Anon, they mustered courage due
　To travel both one way ;
The minister and maiden fair,
　They had their wedding day.

For long they lived together
A happy, married life,
His Reverence and his Lady,
A model man and wife.

———

LOVE, COURTSHIP AND MARRIAGE.

Once on a time a farmer
When tired of single life,
Began in sober earnest
To look out for a wife.

Anon, he saw a maiden
So fair, with sweet brown eyes ;
So charming and so graceful,
And yet so meek and wise.

His thoughts would on her linger,
And love began to spring ;
The gentle chords did vibrate
Like music's choicest string.

He might be a foot taller,
But that no barrier proved ;
His heart moved towards the maiden,
And her's was not unmoved.

True love grew into courtship,
They looked before they leaped ;
If others had done likewise,
They had less sorrow reaped.

This pair of rural courters,
The farmer and his love,
Not only loved each other,
They loved a friend above.

Each heeded Scripture teaching,
 Chose no unequal yoke ;
With them true love and courtship
 Was real, not a joke.

They both were firm abstainers
 From beer, liquor, or wine,
Knowing the wise old proverb—
 " A stitch in time saves nine."

Convinced the goal of drunkards
 Begins with little sups,
They each avoided liquor's
 Intoxicating cups.

In course of time their courtship
 Must rapidly move on ;
Forward they looked with pleasure,
 To being joined in one.

The farmer popped the question,
 She did not say him nay,
For when they were together,
 Time glided sweet away.

A short time after Christmas,
 A many years gone by,
The farmer and his sweetheart
 The marriage knot did tie.

They still glide on together,
 Through good report or ill,
And old-time marriage pledges,
 Yet lovingly fulfil.

Madame attends the dairy,
 Whilst he looks after stock ;
Sometimes they make long hours,
 Scarce watching time or clock.

Anon discoursing music,
  Or singing sweet refrain ;
Hymning Jehovah's praises,
  Their voices tune again.

Still pressing onward, upward,
  Life's journey, hand in hand ;
Hoping through Jesu's merits,
  To gain fair Canaan's land.

SOWING AND REAPING.

Gear up your teams, husbandmen, now—
Horses instruct, both when and how,
And where to till the land and plough.

Gee, ho ! drive on, when all is ready
Set plough the proper depth, and steady
Abreast, now pull, " Captain " and " Neddy."

Hold not your reinings over tight,
Nor with harsh words abuse or fright,
Then turn the furrows left and right.

Scatter the seed at proper time,
Good, well adapted for your clime,
With hands or drill, sow well in line.

The farmer, who good seed doth sow
To fructify and fruitful grow,
Expects same kind to reap, we know.

Oats don't produce barley or wheat,
Or wheat the oats, however neat,
But each its own kind, pure and sweet.

In morals, as we sow we reap ;
In social life this good doth keep,
Reaping oft as we act and speak.

If spiritual things we view,
The Scripture words, holy and true,
Apply to all —both me and you.

Be not deceived, but ponder, know—
Seed good or bad, which here we sow
For future reaping time will grow.

Good seed, all scatter left and right,
At evening, morning, noon-day light,
Till harvest ripens rich and bright.

THE ROACHES & NEIGHBOURHOOD.

The Roaches, with its rocky height,
Some sloping others bold and straight,
Year in and out stands there all right.

Bright summer's sun, cold winter's snow
Can't make the Roaches melt, or go —
Unmoved it stands for friend or foe.

Long years ago, the old Rock Hall—
Betty and David home did call—
Their worldly treasures were but small.

Betty, round with her meal bag went,
Perchance her grandson David lent
Some help— or gathering bilberrys went.

The children oft have played about
With laughter, or with merry shout
Yet this in no way puts it out.

Though numbers come to view it o'er,
It takes it calmly as before—
If learned or simple, rich or poor.

When Prince and Princess Teck once came,
Its modesty was still the same,
Though visited by wealth and fame.

If we would neighbouring history trace,
The changes which have taken place
Might occupy much time and space.

'Neath Roaches base, end, side, or back,
Historians easily might track
Scenes needing not interest to lack.

Young men and maidens who have met,
Did not each other quite forget—
But on each other love did set.

In time they each agreed to wed,
The words " I will" were gladly said —
Anon a curtain lecture read.

But oft the parties of one mind
Have proved, we hope, both true and kind,
And wisdoms' pleasant path did find.

Hen Cloud and Roaches still command
A charming view on either hand
Of hill and dale and meadow land.

They still appear secure and fast,
For many years may stand and last,
Till time's swift tide has hurried past.

THE POTTERIES.

Staffordshire Potteries is now
  A useful, busy place :
Its crockery, we're glad to know,
  Doth English tables grace.

Your dinner services and jugs,
  Choice, ornamented well ;
Variety of pans and mugs—
  Useful, we're pleased to tell.

Good coffee cups and cups for tea,
  Grand patterns and right size,
From which we oft partake with glee
  A beverage we prize.

What progress, truly, has been made
  Since honoured Wedgwood's days ;
Still press along the upward grade
  Of peaceful, prosperous ways.

Let Burslem, Hanley, Fenton, Stoke,
  Environs join as well
In each one's progress be a spoke
  Prosperity to swell.

United, show a firm, bold front
  'Gainst all that's base or wrong ;
To guard, let ever be your wont
  Thoughts, actions, and the tongue.

Each other try to comfort— cheer
  Along the path of right ;
E'er onwards, upwards, march and steer
  To all that's pure and bright.

Staffordshire Potteries we hope
  And wish you good success ;
Still with the times your crockery cope,
  Tables adorn and dress.

KNAVE ALCOHOL.

(Composed for and sung at a Temperance
Meeting in 1895.)

Tune—*Auld Lang Syne.*

Young men and maidens list to me,
  While you a song I sing,
And bid you each and all beware
  Of " Alcohol," the King.

His reign extends from age to age,
  O'er realms of bond and free ;
And still his votaries he bends
  To direst slavery.

He cares not for the widow's tears,
  Or orphan's bitterest cry :
And those who serve the big old Knave,
  Reap sorrow by and bye.

Some seem to think they could not get
  Their crops without the beer :
But let them have the will and then
  The way will be quite clear.

Some boast about the strength they gain
  By drinking beer and gin ;
But I have seen them when, I'm sure,
  It had not strengthened them.

I've seen them when they scarce could stand,
  Or walk along the road :
Or if they did they reeled about,
  They had too big a load.

I've even seen them try their length
  Upon the wet, cold floor ;
And if they had to move a bit,
  They had to use all four.

His subjects thus he overthrows
  And rules them on the floor,
Yet after all their heavy blows,
  They're loyal as before.

(Chorus or Refrain after last verse) :—

  So lads and lasses let's be wise,
    And each decide to-night
  To sign the temperance pledge, and shun
    Old " Alcohol " outright.

———

THANKSGIVING ROW A L.

Don't travel grumbling side walk,
  Dwell in Thanksgiving Row ;
Ne'er give or take offence in talk,
  To anger—all be slow.

Kind words each always favour,
  Actions be pure and bright ;
Right good thoughts ever honour,
  Be thankful day and night.

Husbandmen, do not grumble
  At seasons wet or dry ;
Be thankful, peaceful, humble,
  To alter them don't try.

If wet, it suits the hill sides.
  Stony, or sandy soil ;
If dry, the valley fresh abides
  And flourishing meanwhile.

We view from various standpoints
  Weather. stock, produce, fields ;
Whilst one desires good, fat joints,
  Another pure milk yields.

A third has fields in tillage,
  And ploughs and sows the land ;
The fourth requires grass herbage,
  Stirks gazing on each hand.

Merchants, who deal with farmers,
  Variety require ;
Some, prime, fat cheese or butter,
  Others good beef desire.

Let tradesmen and consumers
  In towns or village, join
With those who are producers,
  In thankfulness sublime.

THE FARMER'S CALENDAR.

The Farmer and his better-half—
  And family as well,
With farm work, dairy cows and calves,
  Of busy hours can tell.

In January snow and frost
  May more or less abound,
Still, never count the time as lost
  Which lightens well the ground.

Manure cart out in February,
  And plough the corn land o'er :
The cattle keep well-warm and dry,
  Dairy feeders and store.

As March progresses sow your seed,
  And harrow well the ground ;
Then roll it if it stands in need,
  And work the fallow ground.

THE FARMER'S CALENDAR *continued*.

In April drop potato sets
  And sow the turnip seed,
Plant cabbage when the weather's wet
  And don't forget the weed.

In May now loose the cattle out
  To grass and herbage sweet,
To pasture and to roam about
  In May they'll find a treat.

In June and every month and day,
  The cattle milk well, please ;
The Dairy, also make it pay,
  Make prime, fat, mellow cheese.

Or otherwise good butter make,
  Or if new milk you sell,
Much care the farmers have to take,
  To do both right and well.

July, gee woa ! horses, machines
  Drive on, the grass cut down :
Make hay while yet the sun doth shine,
  Before it gets too brown.

From early morn till late at night,
  Is harvest working day ;
Yet this we farmers count all right
  If we secure good hay.

August, the corn commence to reap,
  Or badge or mow it down :
The sheaves upend, in kivers heap,
  Then with two hudders crown.

September, cart to stacks or barn
  If drying sunshine come,
And thatch the stack, preserve from harm,
  Then sing glad harvest home.

October, raise potato crops,
　　Sort well and put them by :
The turnips now begin to top,
　　And store them nice and dry.

November, fogs now come apace,
　　Long evenings — damp or cold ;
Inside for cattle make some space,
　　In shed or cowhouse fold.

December, last month of the year,
　　Days are not over long.
On towards the end bright Christmas cheer
　　With pleasant Christian song.

———

ADVICE GRATIS.

" Be ye not unequally yoked."

Young men and maids permit me now,
　　You heartily to greet
A subject you may have in view,
　　On which we now will treat.

Without a fee of six-and-eight,
　　Or even three-and-four ;
Accept advice which may prove good,
　　As if you paid a score.

Young men who farm and till the land,
　　If you require a wife ;
Select a farmer's daughter, as
　　Your helpmate true for life.

Young lady drapers, grocers too,
　　If you should need a husband,
Choose one who weighs and measures well,
　　Then give to him your hand.

93

Young men who make gent.'s coats and vests,
  Needing a change in life,
No doubt a dressmaker by trade,
  Should make a sewing wife.

Young temperance ladies, each be wise,
  A sober husband take :
A toper should not have the prize—
  Don't him your husband make.

Young men who will not steady be,
  Who will not shun the glass,
Don't drag a temperance maiden down—
  Select a tippling lass.

Suffer advice—turn to the right.
  If you would comfort gain :
Each make a firm resolve at once,
  From tippling to abstain.

Christian young men and maidens fair,
  Choose each a Christian mate :
Have no unequal yoke to bear
  In wedlock's holy state.

Each kindly help each other on
  In wisdom's pleasant ways :
Keep step along the happy road,
  Leading to realms of day.

Young men and maidens 'ere we part,
  Or as we say, adieu !
Take our advice, make a wise choice,
  Each keep the end in view.

SURPASSING LOVE.

*"For God so loved the world that He gave His
only begotten Son, that whosoever believeth in Him,
should not perish, but have everlasting life."*—John,
c. iii., v. 6.

How rich, full, and fragrant the love here portrayed
Towards a lost race of sinners displayed :
Our kind, loving Father, in Heaven above,
Here sweetly unfolds the depths of His love.

To ransome—to rescue, redeem, and to save
Mankind the world over, how freely He gave
His only begotten loved Son, to atone
For sinners, to save through His merits alone.

The word "whosoever" includes each and all,
Who hear and accept His free, loving call :
For Jew and for Gentile His love did devise,
Free Gospel salvation, for simple and wise.

Repent and believe on Jesus alone,
Who died on the cross, for sin to atone :
Thus pardon and peace, and freedom accept—
Continue in love—faith ever be kept.

Hope, blooming and full, hold fast and retain,
Safe anchored on Christ, for ever remain :
The Christian believer has happiness here—
The rich promised grace to comfort and cheer.

True Friend, to direct, to counsel and guide
His people who trust Him, and in Him abide ;
So loving, so kind, so tender and true,
Safe shelter and harbour for me and for you.

Then life everlasting— rich pleasures that last
When summers are ended, and seasons are past :
A home with the ransomed—the radiant throng
To sing in sweet harmony Zion's new song.

UNITY,

" Behold, how good and how pleasant a thing it is for brethren to dwell together in unity."

Ps. 132, 1.

The kind words each one speak them,
  The cheerful smiles all give ;
In peace and loving kindness
  Let families all live.
In gentle, loving union,
  Husband and wife combine,
As time glides smoothly onward,
  May love the brighter shine.

O let no mischief maker
  E'er part whom God hath joined ;
Let harsh words never sever
  Those one in heart and mind ;
Let smiles and sunshine ever
  Dwell in our dear sweet homes ;
May hate and envy never
  To England's homesteads come.

Parents and children ever
  Be loving, true and kind :
In Scripture's sacred teaching,
  The perfect model find.
Parents provoke not children,
  But train them day by day
To trust and serve our Saviour,
  The Truth, the Life, the Way.

Children, obey your parents,
  Cheerful your duties do,
Unto them give due honour,
  Be loyal, gentle, true ;
As they advance in years,
  And hoary grows the head :
Love, joy, and peace and gladness,
  Around their pathway spread.

UNITY—*continued.*

Brothers and sisters ever,
    And friends let all agree :
No jarring string let sever
    Sweet kindred harmony.
Let each love one another,
    All cast on Him your care :
Whose love surpasses brothers'
    His love and friendship share.

LONDON.

London of note—of fame—renown
Tip top of every English town,
We often think, hear, read of thee :
Important city, great and free.

There, Parliament doth often meet,
Tories and Whigs each other greet :
Of course they don't quite think alike,
But let each do their duty right.

At times the members sent up there
Scarce keep their promises quite fair :
Just promise on election lines
What you will keep in future times.

The Mayors have there a wondrous show,
In pomp and splendour, off they go :
Perchance it would be better spent
If to the poor some bread were sent.

The people flock from distant towns
The gents in coats, ladies in gowns ;
And country people round about,
To London city oft set out.

To view the city's wondrous scenes,
Where British Kings and British Queens
Were crowned to reign o'er Britishers,
South, east and west, and northerners.

LONDON *continued.*

Far, far across, o'er land and seas
Vast numbers Britain's Queen obey :
Long may she reign o'er loyal hosts —
Three cheers for her, a hearty toast.

The London Tower must be viewed o'er,
Old relics of the days of yore
And the crown jewels may be seen,
Which quite a period there have been.

The Britishers Museum too
Should be examined, well look'd through :
For interesting it must be.
Such vast variety to see.

Madame Tussaud's wax photos see,
Let past and present linked now be ;
Great men, who in the days of yore
Walked London streets. walk there no more.

Preachers and authors, poets, sage,
Of London town from age to age
Come crowding fast into our thoughts,
Great lights, who useful knowledge taught.

Famed churches, chapels, where they preached
Glad gospel tidings free for each ;
Some in the open air did sow
Seeds of the kingdom there to grow.

You sowers also still at work,
Your honest duties never shirk ;
Scatter good seed where'er you go,
Kind words and actions let them grow.

Hail ! London capital renowned,
Where England's sovereigns have been crowned
Prosperity we wish to thee,
Important city, great and free.

FLIRTS.

The boys who at birds stones wantonly whirl,
Remind us of youths who flirt with the girls :
To either young rascals suppose we'd the chance,
We'd scarcely a medal for kindness advance.

We consider the treadmill is nearer the mark
Of what they deserve, who just for a lark
A maiden's affections would wantonly gain :
Then leave in the lurch, causing sorrow or pain.

Young men, who in flirting try pleasure to find,
Permit us to tell you a bit of our mind :
It's unkind, uncalled for, unmanly, unfair,
A credit to no one—a mask thus to wear.

Consider it calmly what would be your views,
If you were a maiden, and stood in her shoes.
What you would like others to do unto you,
Endeavour at all times by all means to do.

Take leisure and think you'll find a wise plan,
Each know your own mind if you possibly can :
Don't leap at a venture, or leap in the dark,
But sail in pure waters affections sweet barque.

Young ladies, don't jilt, keep clean your own skirts,
Then teach them good manners, all frown on the flirts
Prove to them their weakness, you be a strong miss,
Until they've reformed, allow them no kiss.

Perchance this might teach these vain young mankind
To be more staid and better—more thoughtful of mind :
Don't needlessly wound or pain any heart :
Love wisely and well, and from flirting depart.

Remember then boys, at birds do not throw :
Young men and young maidens, be kind when you woo :
In love and in courtship, and marriage, each try
To do unto others, as you'd be done by.

BOOKS AND PAPERS.

Dear me ! what books and papers
  In modern days are sold :
We ought to be some wiser
  Than in the days of old.
We've still the grand old bible,
  Oh ! let its sacred page
Be diligently studied,
  Obeyed by youth and age.

Of other books and papers,
  The basis let it be ;
May they expound its precepts
  In language, simple, free.
Exclude from all your pages,
  A tendency to wrong ;
Let only right be published,
  Prose, poetry, and song.

The lives of useful good men,
  Each ponder and read o'er,
And emulate their labours,
  Add to their number more.
History, and voyage, or travel,
  Recorded let it be—
If worth time, toil, and paper,
  Of people, land, or sea.

Addresses, sermons, lectures,
  Which good and useful be ;
Variety of textures,
  Wide daylight let them see.
Daily or weekly papers,
  And magazines as well ;
Let nothing that defileth
  Upon their pages dwell.

The Times, the Posts, the News's,
  Whatever be their name :
In leaders, prose, or muses,
  Pure simple truth proclaim.

BOOKS AND PAPERS—*continued*.

Weekly or monthly numbers,
  Some have suggestive names —
Count all that's base as lumber,
  Ne'er give it public fame.

Sundays at Home, hours, leisure,
  Observe, improve them well ;
Still don't forget the assemblies
  Where Gospel News they tell :
Sunday and Home Companions,
  Be careful, select well :
Choose such as ever help you
  In purity to dwell.

Churchman and Noncomformist
  In peace and love abide :
Each try to be the noblest,
  Still labouring side by side.
The Christian Age and Herald
  Keep publishing good news ;
Christians should pull together,
  Though varying in some views.

Good Words, Kind and Right Words
  Let all well spoken be :
Recorder and Miscellany
  With early days agree.
Think of a host of others,
  Which should be read and named,
Their matter pure substantial,
  Well worthy to be famed.

Now publishers be careful
  Authors and readers too
Select the wheat and keep it,
  Let all the chaff go through.
The good and true each nation,
  Still publish far and wide :
On Christ, the one foundation,
  Each build and each abide.

DEAR HOME.

Tune—*Home, Sweet Home.*

Dear home of our childhood, we love thee full well,
And on thy fair scenes how delightful to dwell;
There in life's rosy morning we gathered sweet flowers,
And played in the meadows in bright sunny hours.

CHORUS.

Dear home of our youth, it is pleasant to tell
Of those who in old times did love us so well.

Kind parents and friends, some have left us and gone,
Have passed from their labours, away one by one:
Yet still we remember and think o'er and o'er
Of kind loving friends, and seasons of yore.

CHORUS.

Dear home of our youth, it is pleasant to tell
Of those who in old times did love us so well.

Dear home of the present, right gladly we sing,
Of peace and the comfort, pure home life doth bring:
Though duty or business oft calls us from home,
Yet back in the evening with pleasure we come.

CHORUS.

Dear home of the present, though oft called away,
We gladly return at the close of the day.

With pleasure we boast of our dear ones so kind,
So deeply engraven on heart and on mind;
Still travel together life's pilgrimage o'er,
And steer for the port where friends part no more.

CHORUS.

Dear home of the present, though oft called away,
We gladly return at the close of the day.

LUDCHURCH AND RIVER DANE.

Some miles from Leak and Buxton town,
Is Ludchurch place of some renown:
From Macclesfield, Buxton and Leek
Come people out who pleasure seek.

From Manchester and Potteries too,
Friends come this ancient Church to view;
Whilst Liverpool and Congleton
Contingents furnish —looking on.

The country folk too join among.
To see Ludchurch they go along,
On bright and sunny summer weather,
It's nice amongst the flowering heather.

Ludchurch is quite a curious place,
To look at, or its history trace:
It boasts no door at either end,
And over it no roof doth bend.

A wondrous cavern 'twixt the rocks,
Continues there through old time's shocks;
Standing secure, from age to age,
Whilst winters' storms may rush and rage.

From what old people used to tell,
Squire Trafford, loving sport too well,
Once on a time —on hunting bent—
Right smack o'er Ludchurch leaping went.

The bold old outlaw—Robin Hood,
Whose presence there bespoke no good,
Most likely harboured with his men,
Within that wild and rocky glen.

Perchance in persecution's days,
Some met in there, for prayer and praise.
Where they could sing sweet gospel songs,
Away from persecution's wrongs.

Not far from here the river Dane
Two counties' boundaries makes quite plain :
Stafford and Cheshire - parting there
Down in that valley—rustic, fair.

Dane waters glide o'er gravel bed,
Unmindful of the rocks ahead ;
Anon they ripple gaily o'er,
As if in mirth or laughter's roar.

The rural village of Danebridge
Is grand with trees and dale and ridge :
The river, rushing on between.
Wild flowers and herbs, and grasses green.

MERRY MAY.

Bright May, with genial sunshine,
Again we welcome thee,
As in the days of childhood
When life was full of glee.
The sun is just as radient,
As when we romped about
Amongst the grass and Daisies,
With merry laugh and shout.

How oft we searched the hedges,
For nest of Finch or Lark,
Anon by feathered songsters
Sometimes constrained to hark.
Perchance the broody Lapwing
Called "pe-wit" over head
Then on a distance farther
A large bird "cuckoo" said.

MERRY MAY—*continued.*

The Corncreak rather harshly
Its note did often raise :
Anon the Lark or Linnet
Would warble sweeter lays.
The Blackbird and the Throstle,
Sounded their tune abroad.
Others with chirp or whistle
Twittered with one accord.

The lovely pure wild flowers,
Studded the ditch and field,
How nice and sweet the fragrance
Which some of them did yield,
Since then though many seasons
And Mays have hurried past,
Thy sunny hours are pleasant,
And cheerful while they last.

Though many things have altered,
And we have older grown,
And don't feel quite as active,
Now, as of yore. we own.
The birds still warble sweetly,
The flowers are fragrant—gay,
As when we first did greet thee,
Bright, cheerful. merry May.

THE BEAUTIES OF NATURE
IN JUNE.

See the beauties of our world,
In its summer dress unfurled ;
Lovely are the garden flowers,
Relic of fair Eden's bowers.

Fruit trees, hedge rows, in their bloom,
Into fruit emerging soon :
Fragrant now, and pure and sweet,
And the fruit, when ripe, a treat.

Mountains, valleys, decked in green,
How enchanting now they seem ;
Pleasant is a mountain walk,
With kind friends to chat and talk.

Pleasant too the charming vales
Where the rippling waters trail ;
Fishes, in their happy glee,
Leaping actively, now see.

Meadow grass progresses now,
Sweet wild flowers are just in glow :
Bright green blades of springing corn,
Dew drops sparkling— bright June morn.

Cattle now repose at rest,
On the grounds herb spangled breast,
And when rested well they eat
Fresh sweet grass—to them a treat.

East and west, and south and north,
Little birds are warbling forth ;
Pleasure to mankind they bring,
As in harmony they sing.

THE DIAMOND JUBILEE.

Tune—*National Anthem.*

The Diamond Jubilee,
Let Britain's sons so free,
    And daughters too.
Now hail with joy and glee,
This long reign— jubilee !
Her reign continued be ;
    God bless our Queen.

Let this grand jubilee
Long, long remembered be,
    All o'er our land,
The poor, let them be fed,
Only kind words be said,
Widow and orphan's head
    With plenty crown.

Long may England's loved Queen
O'er loyal subjects reign,
    In honour bright.
On this grand jubilee
Let people all agree
Each sing in faithful glee
    God bless our Queen.

This Diamond Jubilee,
All England hails with glee,
    Colonies join.
Let all the human kind
In fellowship be joined
Sing with one heart and mind
    God bless our Queen.

GOD BLESS OUR HOMES.

Tune—*National Anthem*

In favoured England's homes,
Love, joy and peace e'er come,
    God bless our homes.
Comfort the sick and sad,
Sweet melody be had,
Let Britain's homes be glad,
    God bless our homes.

Affections sweet, unriven,
Smiles and kind looks be given
    In our dear homes.
Husbands and wifes agree,
Children parents obey,
Base thoughts or actions flee
    From English homes.

True pleasures e'er be found,
Still grow, increase, abound,
    Make home life glad.
Sing cheerful Christian lays,
Walk wisdom's pleasant ways,
Enjoying happy days
    In Christian homes.

Father in heaven bless,
Clothe with Thy righteousness
    Earth's daughters' sons.
Thy grace, and love, and light,
Shed on our pathway bright,
Guide all Thy people right,
    God bless our homes.—Amen.

FINIS.

www.ingramcontent.com/pod-product-compliance
Lightning Source LLC
Chambersburg PA
CBHW022341020726
47500CB00004B/1225